I'm royal and there'll be a worldwide search...

He couldn't tell her.

For some unknown reason, a voice in the back of his head was pleading "not yet." She thought he was an equal. A soldier, nothing more.

She'd been battered by people who'd treated her as trash. She was feisty and brave, but she'd retreated to this island, hurt.

He didn't want her retreating from him. He knew he'd have to tell her, but the voice was almost yelling.

Not yet. Not yet.

Dear Reader,

Stepping into the Prince's World started life in my dentist's waiting room. The dentist surgery is understandably not my favorite place to visit, but with a lovely pile of glossies I can block out the thought of what's ahead. I flicked through the pages, looking at pictures of a certain soldier/prince and thought, what a combination!

And suddenly I was off and dreaming. By the time I was escorted into the dentist chair I had my own soldier/prince in my head, and a heroine who deserved him. I had shipwrecks and deserted islands, I had chandeliers and tiaras, I had my own kingdom—all I had to do was get rid of one small dental cavity, escape the dentist and go write a book.

Welcome to Claire and Raoul's world. Enjoy.

Marion

Stepping into the Prince's World

Marion Lennox

—

Marion Lennox

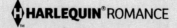
HARLEQUIN® ROMANCE

Recycling programs
for this product may
not exist in your area.

ISBN-13: 978-0-373-74400-8

Stepping into the Prince's World

First North American publication 2016

Printed in U.S.A.

Marion Lennox has written more than a hundred romances and is published in over a hundred countries and thirty languages. Her multiple awards include the prestigious RITA® Award (twice), and the *RT Book Reviews* Career Achievement Award for "a body of work which makes us laugh and teaches us about love."

Marion adores her family, her kayak, her dog, and lying on the beach with a book someone else has written. Heaven!

Books by Marion Lennox

Harlequin Romance

The Logan Twins

Nine Months to Change His Life

The Larkville Legacy

Taming the Brooding Cattleman

Sparks Fly with the Billionaire
Christmas at the Castle
Christmas Where They Belong
The Earl's Convenient Wife

Visit the Author Profile page
at Harlequin.com for more titles.

For Doug and Natalia.
Wishing you a fabulous wedding and an
amazing, fulfilling Happy Ever After.
Welcome home.

With grateful thanks to Jennifer Kloester
who certainly knows where and how to kick.
If our Jen met a prince on a dark night,
she'd know what to do. :-)

CHAPTER ONE

YOU'RE TO TAKE your place as heir to the throne and find yourself a bride.

If Crown Prince Raoul Marcus Louis Ferdinand could cut that last order from his grandmother's letter he would, but he needed to show his commanding officer the letter in its entirety.

He laid the impressive parchment of his grandmother's letter before his commanding officer. Franz noted the grim lines on Raoul's face, picked up the letter and read.

Then he nodded. 'You have no choice,' he told him.

'I don't.' Raoul turned and stared out of the window at the massive mountain overshadowing Tasmania's capital. It was a mere shadow of the mountains of Marétal's alpine region.

He needed to be home.

'I've known my grandfather's health is failing,' he told his commanding officer. 'But I've always thought of the Queen as invincible. This letter might sound commanding, but it's a plea for help.'

'It is.' Franz glanced at the letter again. It was headed by the royal crest of Marétal and it wasn't a letter to be ignored. A royal summons... 'But at least it's timely,' he told Raoul.

Marétal's army had been engaged as part of an international exercise in Tasmania's wilderness for the last couple of months. Raoul's battalion had performed brilliantly, but operations were winding down.

'We can manage without you,' he told him. He hesitated. 'Raoul, you do know…?'

'That it's time I left the army.' Raoul sighed. 'I do know it. But my grandmother effectively runs the kingdom.'

'The Queen's seventy-six.'

'Tell *her* that.' He shook his head at the thought of his indomitable grandmother. His grandfather, King Marcus, even though officially ruler, hardly emerged from his library. Queen Alicia had more or less run the country since the day she'd married, and she suffered no interference. But she was asking for help now.

'Of course you're right,' he continued. 'My grandparents' chief aide, Henri, has written privately that he's worried about the decisions my grandmother's taking. Or not taking. Our health and legal systems need dragging into this century. More immediately, national security seems to be an issue. Henri tells me of threats which she refuses to take seriously. He suggests increasing the security service, making it a force to be reckoned with, but the Queen sees no need.'

'You're just the man to do it.'

'I've never been permitted to change anything,'

Raoul said flatly. 'And now…' He turned back to Franz's desk and stared morosely at the letter. '*This*. She wants me home for the ball to celebrate her fifty years on the throne.'

'It'll be a splendid occasion,' Franz told him. He, too, glanced back at the letter—particularly at the last paragraph—and try as he might he couldn't suppress a grin.

'You think it's *funny*?' Commanding officer or not, Franz copped a glare from Raoul. 'That the Queen decrees I bring a suitable partner or she'll provide me with one herself?'

'She wants to see you married, with an heir to the throne. She fears for you and the monarchy otherwise.'

'She wants me under her thumb, with a nice aristocratic bride to match.'

'You've never been under her thumb before.'

Franz had known Prince Raoul ever since he'd joined the army. Raoul presented to the world as the perfect Prince, the perfect grandson, but Franz knew that underneath his mild exterior Raoul did exactly what he wanted. If the Queen had known half of what her grandson had been doing in the army she'd have called him home long since.

But therein lay the success of their relationship. To his grandmother, Raoul was a young man who smiled sweetly and seemed to agree with whatever she decreed. *'Yes, Grandmama, I'm sure you're right.'* Raoul never made promises he couldn't keep, but he certainly knew the way to get what he wanted.

'Our people will approve of me in military uniform,' he'd told the Queen when he'd announced his decision to join the army. 'It's a good look, Grandmama—the Crown Prince working for the country rather than playing a purely ceremonial role. With your approval I'll join the Special Forces. Have you seen their berets? It can do the royal image nothing but good.'

His grandmother had had to agree that his military uniform suited him. So had the country's media. At thirty five, with his height, his jet-black hair, his tanned skin and the hooded grey eyes that seemed almost hawk-like, the added 'toughness' of his uniform made the tabloids go wild every time they had the opportunity to photograph him.

'His uniform makes him look larger,' the Queen had told a journalist when Raoul had completed his first overseas posting.

Franz had read the article and thought of the years of gruelling physical training turning Raoul into a honed Special Forces soldier. His admiration for his royal charge had increased with every year he knew him.

Now he came round and gripped his shoulder. Franz had been Raoul's first commanding officer when he'd joined the army fifteen years ago. As Raoul had risen up the ranks so had Franz, and over the years they'd become friends.

'If you were a normal officer you'd be taking my place when I retire next year,' Franz told him. 'The army wouldn't give you a choice and that'd mean desk work. You know you hate desk work. There's so much more you can do working as heir to the throne—and you'll wear a much prettier uniform.'

Raoul told him where he could put his uniform and the older man chuckled.

'Yes, but you'll be wearing tassels, lad, and maybe even a sabre. There's a lot to be said for tassels and sabres. When do you need to leave?'

'The ball's in a month.'

'But you need to leave before that.' Franz glanced at the letter and his lips twitched again. 'According to this you have a spot of courting to do before you get there. First find your bride...'

Raoul rolled his eyes.

'I may have to go home,' he said carefully. 'I may even have to take up the duties of Crown Prince. But there's no way my grandmother can make me marry.'

'Well,' Franz said, and grinned again, 'I know Her Majesty. Good luck.'

Raoul said nothing. Some comments weren't worth wasting breath on.

Franz saw it and moved on to practicalities. 'Let's consider you on leave from now,' he told him. 'We'll work out discharge plans later. You can fly out tonight if you want.'

'I don't want to fly out tonight.'

'What *do* you want?'

'Space,' Raoul told him. 'Space to get my head around what I'm facing. But you're right. I need to go home. My grandparents are failing. I know my country needs me. I *will* go home—but not to find a bride.'

If she edged any closer to the end of the world she might fall off.

Claire Tremaine sat on the very highest cliff on the highest headland of Orcas Island and thumbed her nose in the direction of Sydney. It was Monday morning. In the high-rise offices of Craybourne, Ledger and Smythe, scores of dark-suited legal eagles would be poring over dull documents, checking the ASIC indexes, discussing the Dow Jones, making themselves their fifth or sixth coffee of the morning.

She was so much better off here.

Or not.

She sort of…*missed* it.

Okay, not most of it—but, oh, she missed the coffee.

And she was just ever so frightened of storms. And just a bit isolated.

Would there be a storm? The forecast was saying a weather front was moving well east of Tasmania. There was no mention of it turning towards Orcas Island, but Claire had been on the island for four months now, and was starting to recognise the wisps of cloud formation low on the horizon that spelled trouble.

A storm back in Sydney had meant an umbrella and delays on the way home to her bedsit. A storm on Orcas Island could mean she was shut in the house for days. There was a reason the owners of this island abandoned it for six months of the year. This was a barren, rocky outcrop, halfway between Victoria and Tasmania, and the sea here was the wildest in the world. In the worst of the storms Claire couldn't even stand up in the wind.

'But that's what we put our names down for,' she told Rocky, the stubby little fox terrier she'd picked up on impulse from the animal shelter the day she'd left to come here. 'Six months of isolation to get to know each other and to forget about the rest of the world.'

But the rest of the world had decent coffee.

The supply boat wasn't due for another week, and even then on its last visit they'd substituted her desired brand with a no-name caterers' blend.

Sigh.

'Two more months to go,' she told Rocky, and rose and stared out at the gathering clouds.

To come here had been a spur-of-the-moment decision, and she'd had plenty of time to regret it. She was looking at the rolling clouds and regretting it now.

'I'm sure the weather forecast's wrong,' she told her dog. 'But let's go batten down the hatches, just in case.'

He should tell someone where he was going.

If he did his bodyguards would join him. That was the deal. When he was working within his army unit his bodyguards backed off. As soon as he wasn't surrounded by soldiers, his competent security section took over.

Only they didn't treat him as a colleague. They treated him as a royal prince who needed to be protected—not only from outside harm but from doing anything that might in any way jeopardise the heir to the throne of Marétal.

Like going sailing on his own.

But he hadn't let them know he was on leave yet. As far as they were concerned he was still on military exercises, so for now he was free of their watch. He'd walked straight from Franz's office down to the docks. He was still wearing his military uniform. In a city full of army personnel, based here for multinational exercises, his uniform gave him some degree of anonymity. That anonymity wouldn't last, he knew. As soon as he shed his uniform, as soon as he went home, he'd be Crown Prince forever.

But *not* married to a woman of his grandmother's choosing, he thought grimly. He knew the women she thought suitable and he shuddered.

And then he reached *Rosebud*, the neat little yacht

he'd been heading for, and forgot about choosing a bride.

This was Tom Radley's yacht. Tom was a local army officer and Raoul had met him on the first part of their combined international operation. They'd shared an excellent army exercise, abseiling across 'enemy territory' in some of Tasmania's wildest country. Friendships were forged during such ordeals, and the men had clicked.

'Come sailing with me when we're back in Hobart,' Tom had said, and they'd spent a great afternoon on the water.

But Tom had been due to take leave before the exercises had ended, and a mountain in Nepal had beckoned. Before he'd gone he'd tossed the keys of the yacht to Raoul.

'Use her, if you like, while you're still in Tasmania,' he'd said diffidently. 'I've seen your skill and I know you well enough now to trust you. I also know how surrounded you are. Just slip away and have a sail whenever you can.'

The little yacht wasn't state-of-the-art. She was a solid tub of a wooden yacht, built maybe forty years ago, sensible and sturdy. Three weeks ago he and Tom had put up a bit too much sail for the brisk conditions, and they'd had fun trying to keep her under control.

And now... Conditions on the harbour were bright, with enough sun to warm the early spring air and a breeze springing up from the south. Clouds were scudding on the horizon. It was excellent sailing weather.

He didn't want to go back to base yet. He didn't want to change out of his uniform, pack his kit and head for home.

He should tell someone where he was going.

'It's only an afternoon's sail,' he said out loud. 'And after today I'll have a lifetime of telling people where I'm going.'

He should still tell someone. Common sense dictated it.

But he didn't want his bodyguards.

'I'll tell them tomorrow,' he said. 'For today I owe no duty to the army. I owe no duty to my country. For today I'm on my own.'

Prince Raoul's movements were supposed to be tracked every step of his life. But it drove Raoul nuts.

Even his afternoon's sail with Tom had been tracked. Because he'd been off duty that weekend, his bodyguards had moved into surveillance mode. He and Tom had had a great time, but even Tom had been unsettled by the motorboat cruising casually within helping distance.

'I couldn't bear it,' Tom had said frankly, and Raoul had said nothing because it was just the way things were.

But this afternoon was different. No one knew he was on leave. No one knew he was looking at Tom's boat and thinking, *Duty starts tomorrow.*

No one saw him slip the moorings and sail quietly out of the harbour.

And no one was yet predicting the gathering storm.

'I'm sure it's a storm,' she told Rocky. 'I don't care what the weather men are saying. I trust my nose.'

Clare was working methodically around the outside of the house, closing the great wooden shutters that protected every window. This house was a mansion—a fantastical whim built by a Melbourne-based billionaire financier who'd fancied his own island with its own helicopter pad so he could fly in whenever he wished.

He'd never wish to be here now, Claire thought as she battened down the house. In the worst of the Bass Strait storms, stones that almost qualified as rocks were hurled against the house.

In the early days, Mrs Billionaire had planted a rose garden to the north of the house. It had looked stunning for half of one summer, but then a storm had hit and her rose bushes had last been seen flying towards the Antarctic. It had then been decided that an Italian marble terrace would look just as good, although even that was now pitted from flying debris.

'I hope I'm imagining things,' she told Rocky. Rocky was sniffing for lizards under the carefully arranged rock formations that during summer visits formed a beautiful 'natural' waterfall. 'The forecast's still for calm.'

But then she looked again at those clouds. She'd been caught before.

'If we lose sun for a couple of days we might even lose power. I might do some cooking in case,' she told Rocky.

Rocky looked up at her and his whole body gave a wriggle of delight. He hadn't been with her for two weeks before he'd realised the significance of the word 'cooking'.

She grinned and picked him up. 'Yes, we will,' she told him. 'Rocky, I'm very glad I have you.'

He was all she had.

She'd been totally isolated when she'd left Sydney. There'd been people in the firm she'd thought were her friends, but she'd been contacted by no one. The whispers had been vicious, and who wanted to be stained by association?

Enough.

She closed her eyes and hugged her little dog. 'Choc chip cookies for me and doggy treats for you,' she told him. 'Friends stick together, and that's you and me. That's what this six months is all about. Learning that we need nobody else.'

The wind swept in from the south—a wind so fierce that it took the meteorologists by surprise. It took Tasmania's fishing fleet by surprise, and it stretched the emergency services to the limit. To say it took

Raoul's unprepared little yacht by surprise was an understatement.

Raoul was an excellent yachtsman. What his skills needed, though, was a thoroughly seaworthy boat to match them.

He didn't have one.

For a while he used the storm jib, trying to use the wind to keep some semblance of control. Then a massive wave crested and broke right over him, rolling the boat as if it was tumbleweed. The little boat self-righted. Raoul had clipped on lifelines. He was safe—for now—but the sail was shredded.

And that was the end of his illusion of control.

He was tossed wherever the wind and the sea dictated. All he could do was hold on and wait for the weather to abate. And hope it did so before *Rosebud* disintegrated and left him to the mercy of the sea.

CHAPTER TWO

Two days into the worst storm to have hit the island since the start of her stay Claire was going stir-crazy. She hadn't been able to step outside once. The wind was so strong that a couple of times she'd seriously worried that the whole house might be picked up.

'You and me, Rocky,' she'd told him, when he'd whimpered at the sound of the wind roaring across the island. 'Like Dorothy and Toto. When we fly, we'll fly together.'

Thankfully they hadn't flown, and finally the wind was starting to settle. The sun was starting to peep through the clouds and she thought she might just venture out and see the damage.

She quite liked a good storm—as long as it didn't threaten to carry her into the Antarctic.

So she rugged up, and made Rocky wear the dinky little dog coat that he hated but she thought looked cute, and they headed out together.

As soon as she opened the door she thought about retreating, but Rocky was tearing out into the wind, joyful at being allowed outside, heading for his favourite place in the world. The beach.

The sea would look fantastic. She just had to get close enough to the beach to see it. The sea mist

was so heavy she could scarcely see through it—
or was it foam blasted up by the wind? She could
scarcely push against it.

But she was outside. The wind wasn't so strong
that it was hurling stones. She could put her head
down and fight it.

Below the house was a tiny cove—a swimming
beach in decent weather. She headed there now, expecting to see massive damage, expecting to see…

A boat?

Or part of a boat.

She stopped, so appalled she almost forgot to
breathe. A boat was smashed and part submerged
on the rocks just past the headland.

The boat wasn't big. A weekend sailor? It must
have been trying to reach the relative safety of
the beach, manoeuvring into the narrow channel
of deep water, but the seas would have been overwhelming, driving it onto the rocks.

Dear God, was there anyone…?

And almost as soon as she thought it she saw
a flash of yellow in the water, far out, between
the rocks and the beach. A figure was struggling
through the waves breaking around the rocks.

Whoa.

Claire knew these waters, even thoughtshe'd
never swum here. She'd skimmed stones and
watched the tide in calm weather. She knew there
was a rip, starting from the beach and swinging
outward.

The swimmer was headed straight into it. If he was to have any chance he had to swim sideways, towards the edge of the cove, then turn and swim beside the rip rather than in it.

But he was too far away to hear if she yelled. The wind was still howling across the clifftops, drowning any hope of her being heard.

Was she a heroine?

'I'm not,' she said out loud. But some things weren't negotiable. She couldn't watch him drown—not when she knew the water. And she was a decent swimmer.

'You know where the dog food is, and the back door's open,' she told Rocky as she hauled off her coat and kicked off her boots. 'If I disappear just chew a hole in the sack. Tell 'em I died trying.'

But she had no intention of dying. She'd stick within reach of the rocks, where the current was weakest. She was not a heroine.

Her jeans hit the clothes pile, and then her windcheater. *Okay, then—ready, set, go.*

He was making no headway. The current was hauling him out faster than he could swim.

Raoul had been born tough and trained tougher. He hadn't reached where he was in the army without survival skills being piled on to survival skills. He couldn't outswim the current, so he knew he had to let it carry him out until it weakened—and then he had to figure out a way back in again.

The problem was, he was past exhaustion.

By the time he'd reached this island the yacht had been little more than a floating tub. The torn sails were useless. He'd used the motor to try and find some place to land, but the motor hadn't had the strength to fight the surf. Then a wave, bigger than the rest, had hit him broadside.

The boat had landed upside down on the rocks. He'd hit his head. It had taken him too long to get free of the wreck and now the water was freezing.

If he let the current carry him out, would he have the strength to get back in again?

He had no choice. He forced his body to relax and felt the rip take him. For the first time he stopped trying to swim. He raised his head, looking hopelessly towards the shore. He was being carried out again.

There was someone on the beach.

Someone who could help?

Or not.

The figure was slight—a boy? No, it was a woman, her shoulder-length curls flying out around her shoulders in the wind. She had a dog and she was yelling. She was gesticulating to the east of the cove.

She was ripping off her windcheater and running down to the surf. Heading to the far left of the beach.

If this was a local she'd know the water. She was heading to the left and waving at him.

Maybe that was where the rip cut out.

She was running into the water. She shouldn't risk herself.

He tried to yell but he was past it. He was pretty much past anything.

The woman was running through the shallows and then diving into the first wave that was over chest high. Of all the stupid... Of all the brave...

Okay, if she was headed into peril on his behalf the least he could do was help.

He fought for one last burst of energy. He put his head down and tried to swim.

Uh-oh.

There'd been a swimming pool in the basement of the offices of Craybourne, Ledger and Smythe. Some lawyers swam every lunchtime.

Claire had mostly shopped. Or eaten lunch in the park. Or done nothing at all, which had sometimes seemed a pretty good option.

It didn't seem a good option now. She should have used that time to improve her swimming. She needed to be super-fit or more. There was no rip where she was swimming, but the downside of keeping close to the rocks at the side of the cove was the rocks themselves. They were sharp, and the waves weren't regular. A couple picked her up and hurled her sideways.

She was having trouble fighting her way out. She was also bone-chillingly cold. The iciness of Bass

Strait in early spring was almost enough to give her a heart attack.

And she couldn't see whoever it was she was trying to rescue.

He must be here somewhere, she thought. She just had to fight her way out behind the surf so she could see.

Which meant diving through more waves. Which meant avoiding more rocks. Which meant...

Crashing.

Something hit him—hard.

He'd already hit his head on the rocks. The world was feeling a bit off-balance anyway. The new crack on his head made him reel. He reached out instinctively to grab whatever it was that had hit him— and it was soft and yielding. A woman. Somehow he tugged her to face him. Her chestnut curls were tangled, her green eyes were blurred with water, and she looked almost as dazed as he was.

He'd thumped his head and so had she. She stared at him, and then she fought to speak.

'You'd think...' She was struggling for breath as waves surged around them but she managed to gasp the words. 'You'd think a guy with the whole of Bass Strait to swim in could avoid my head.'

He had hold of her shoulders—not clutching, just linking himself with her so the wash of the waves couldn't push them apart. They were both in deadly peril, and weirdly his first urge was to laugh. She'd reached him and she was *joking*?

Um… Get safe first. Laugh second.

'*Revenir à la plage. Je suivrai,*' he gasped, and then realised he'd spoken in French, Marétal's official language. Which would be no use at all in Tasmania's icy waters. *Get back to the beach. I'll follow,* he'd wanted to say, and he tried to force his thick tongue to make the words. But it seemed she'd already understood.

'How can you follow? You're drowning.' She'd replied in French, with only a slight haltingness to show French wasn't her first language.

'I'm not.' He had his English together now. And his tongue almost working.

'There's blood on your head,' she managed.

'I'm okay. You've shown me the way. Put your head down and swim. I'm following.'

'Is there anyone…?' The indignation and her attempt at humour had gone from her voice and fear had replaced it. She was gasping between waves. 'Is there anyone else in the boat?'

Anyone else to save? She'd dived into the water to save him and was now proposing to head out further and save others?

This was pure grit. His army instructors would be proud of her.

She didn't have a lifejacket on and he did.

'No one,' he growled. 'Get back to the beach.'

'You're sure?'

'I'm sure. Go.' He should make *her* wear the life jacket, but the effort of taking the thing off was beyond him.

'Don't you dare drown. I've taken too much trouble.'

'I won't drown,' he managed, and then a wave caught her and flung her sideways.

She hit the closest rock and disappeared. He tried to grab her but she was under water—gone.

Hell...

He dived, adrenalin surging, giving him energy when he'd thought he had none. And then he grabbed and caught something...

A wisp of lace. He tugged and she was free of the rocks, back in his arms, dazed into limpness.

He fought back from the rocks and tried to steady while she fought to recover.

'W...wow,' she gasped at last. 'Sorry. I...you can let go now.'

'I'm not letting go.' But he shifted his grip. He'd realised what he'd been holding were her knickers. He now had hold of her by her bra!

'We surf in together,' he gasped. 'I have a lifejacket. I'm not letting go.'

'You...can't...'

He heard pain in her voice.

'You're hurt.'

'There's no way I can put a sticking plaster on out here,' she gasped. 'Go.'

'We go together.'

'You'll stretch my bra,' she gasped, and once again he was caught by the sheer guts of the woman. She was hurt, she was in deadly peril, and she was trying to make him smile.

'Yeah,' he told her. 'And if it stretches too far I'll get an eyeful—but not until we're safe on the beach. Just turn and kick.'

'I'll try,' she managed, and then there was no room for more words. There was only room to try and live.

She couldn't actually swim.

There was something wrong with her arm. Or her shoulder? Or her chest? She wasn't sure where the pain was radiating from, but it was surely radiating. It was the arm furthest from him—if he'd been holding her bra on that side she might have screamed. If she *could* scream without swallowing a bucket of seawater. Unlikely, she thought, and then wondered if she was making sense. She decided she wasn't but she didn't care.

She had to kick. There was no way she'd go under. She'd risked her life to save this guy and now it seemed he didn't need saving. Her drowning would be a complete waste.

Some people would be pleased.

And there was a thought to make her put her head down, hold her injured arm to her side as much as she could and try to kick her way through the surf.

She had help. The guy still had his hand through

her bra, holding fast. His kick was more powerful than hers could ever be. But he still didn't know this beach.

'Keep close to the rocks,' she gasped during a break in the waves. 'If you don't stay close you'll be caught in the rip.'

'Got it,' he told her. 'Now, shut up and kick.'

And then another wave caught them and she had the sense to put her head down and kick, even if the pain in her shoulder was pretty close to knocking her out. And he kicked too, and they surged in, and suddenly she was on sand. The wave was ripping back out again but the guy was on his feet, tugging her up through the shallows.

'We're here,' he gasped. 'Come on, lady, six feet to go. You can do it.'

And she'd done it. Rocky was tearing down the beach to meet them, barking hysterically at the stranger.

Enough. She subsided onto the sand, grabbed Rocky with her good arm, held him tight and burst into tears.

For a good while neither of them moved.

She lay on the wet sand and hugged her dog and thought vaguely that she had to make an effort. She had to get into dry clothes. She was freezing. And shouldn't she try to see if something was wrong with the guy beside her? He'd slumped down on the sand, too. She could see his chest rise and fall.

He was alive, but his eyes were closed. The weak sunshine was on his unshaven face and he seemed to be drinking it up.

Who was he?

He was wearing army issue camouflage gear. It was the standard work wear of a soldier, though maybe slightly different from the Australian uniform.

He was missing his boots.

Why notice that?

She was noticing his face, too. Well, why not? Even the pain in her shoulder didn't stop her noticing his face.

There was a trickle of blood mixing with the seawater dripping from his head.

He was beautiful.

It was the strongest face she'd ever seen. His features were lean, aquiline...aristocratic? He had dark hair—deep black. It was cropped into an army cut, but no style apart from a complete shave could disguise its tendency to curl. His grey eyes were deep-set and shadowed and he was wearing a couple of days' stubble. He looked beyond exhausted.

She guessed he was in his mid-thirties, and she thought he looked mean.

Mean?

Mean in the trained sense, she corrected herself. Mean as in a lean, mean fighting machine.

She thought, weirdly, of a kid she'd gone to school with. Andy had been a friend with the same ambitions she'd had: to get away from Kunamungle and *be* someone.

'I'll join the army and be a lean, mean fighting machine,' he'd told her.

Last she'd heard, Andy was married with three kids, running the stock and station agents in Kunamungle. He was yet another kid who'd tried to leave his roots and failed.

Her thoughts were drifting in a weird kind of consciousness that was somehow about blocking pain. Something had happened to her arm. Something bad. She didn't want to look. She just wanted to stay still for a moment longer and hold Rocky and think about anything other than what would happen when she had to move.

'Tell me what's wrong?'

He'd stirred. He was pushing himself up, looking down at her in concern.

'H...hi,' she managed, and his eyes narrowed.

Um...where was her bra? It was down around her waist, that was where it was, but she didn't seem to have the energy to do anything about it. She hugged Rocky a bit closer, thinking he'd do as camouflage. If he didn't, she didn't have the strength to care.

'Your arm,' he said carefully, as if he didn't want to scare her.

She thought about that for a bit. Her arm...

'There...there does seem to be a problem. I hit the rocks. I guess I don't make the grade as a lifesaver, huh?'

'If you hadn't come out I'd be dead,' he told her. 'I couldn't fight the rip and I didn't know where it ended.'

'I was trying to signal but I didn't know if you'd seen me.' She was still having trouble getting her voice to work but it seemed he was, too. His lilting accent—French?—was husky, and she could hear exhaustion behind it. He had been in peril, she thought. Maybe she *had* saved him. It was small consolation for the way her arm felt, but at least it was something.

'Where can I go to get help?' he asked, cautious now, as if he wasn't sure he wanted to know the answer.

'Help?'

'The charts say this island is uninhabited.'

'It's not,' she told him.

'No?'

'There's Rocky and me, and now there's you.'

'Rocky?'

'I'm holding him.'

Silence. Although it wasn't exactly silence. The waves were pounding the sand and the wind was whistling around the cliffs. A stray piece of seaweed whipped past her face like a physical slap.

What was wrong with her arm? She tried a tentative wiggle and decided she wouldn't do *that* again in a hurry.

'Do you live here?'

'I caretake,' she said, enunciating every syllable with care because it seemed important.

'You caretake the island?'

'The house.'

'There's a house?'

'A big house.'

'Excellent,' he told her.

He rose and stared round the beach, then left her with Rocky. Two minutes later he was back, holding her pile of discarded clothes.

'Let's get you warm. You need to put these on.'

'You're wet, too' she told him.

'Yeah, but I don't have a set of dry clothes on the beach. Let's cope with one lot of hypothermia instead of two. Tug your knickers off and I'll help you on with your jeans and windcheater.'

'I'm not taking my knickers off!'

'They're soaked and you're freezing.'

'I have my dignity.'

'And I'm not putting up with misplaced modesty on my watch.' He was holding up her windcheater. 'Over your head with this. Don't try and put your arm in it.'

He slid the windcheater over her head. It was long enough to give her a semblance of respectability as she kicked off her soggy knickers—but not much. She should be wearing wisps of sexy silk, she thought, but she was on an island in winter for six months with no expected company. Her knickers were good solid knickers, bought for warmth, with just a touch of lace.

'My granny once told me to always wear good knickers in case I'm hit by a bus,' she managed. Her teeth were chattering. She had her good arm on his shoulder while he was holding her jeans for her to step into.

'Sensible Granny.'

'I think she meant G-strings with French lace,' she told him. 'Granny had visions of me marrying a doctor. Or similar.'

'Still sensible Granny.' He was hauling her jeans up as if this was something he did every day of the week. Which he surely didn't. He was definitely wearing army issue camouflage. It was soaking. One sleeve was ripped but it still looked serviceable.

He looked capable. Capable of hauling her jeans up and not looking?

Don't go there.

'Why…? Why sensible?' she managed.

'Because we could use a doctor right now,' he told her. 'Your arm…'

'My arm will be fine. I must have wrenched it.' She stared down. He was holding her boots. He must have unlaced them. She'd hauled them off and run.

She took the greatest care to put her feet into them, one after the other, and then tried not to be self-conscious as he tied the laces for her.

She was an awesome lifesaver, she thought ruefully. *Not.*

'Now,' he said, and he took her good arm under the elbow. Rocky was turning crazy circles around them, totally unaware of drama, knowing only that he was out of the house and free. 'Let's get to this house. Is it far?'

'A hundred yards as the crow flies,' she told him. 'Sadly we don't have wings.'

'You mean it's up?'

'It's up.'

'I'm sorry.' For the first time his voice faltered. 'I don't think I can carry you.'

'Well, there's a relief,' she managed. 'Because I might have been forced to let you help me dress, but that's as far as it goes. You're carrying me nowhere.'

It had been two days since he'd set off from Hobart, and to say he was exhausted was an understatement. The storm had blown up from nowhere and the boat's engine hadn't been big enough to fight it. Sails had been impossible. He'd been forced to simply ride it out, trying to use the storm jib to keep clear of land, letting the elements take him where they willed.

And no one knew where he was.

His first inkling of the storm had been a faint black streak on the horizon. The streak had turned into a mass with frightening speed. He'd been a good couple of hours out. As soon as he'd noticed it he'd headed for port, but the storm had overwhelmed him.

And he'd been stupidly unprepared. He'd had his phone, but the first massive wave breaking over the bow had soaked him and rendered his phone useless. He'd kicked himself for not putting it in a waterproof container and headed below to Tom's radio. And found it useless. Out of order.

Raoul had thought then how great Tom's devil-may-care attitude had seemed when he and Tom had done their Sunday afternoon sail with his bodyguard in the background, and how dumb it seemed now. And where was the EPIRB? The emergency position indicating radio beacon all boats should carry to alert the authorities if they were in distress and send an automatic location beacon? Did Tom even own one?

Apparently not.

Dumb was the word to describe what he'd done. He'd set out to sea because he was fed up with the world and wanted some time to himself to reflect. But he wasn't so fed up that he wanted to die, and with no one knowing where he was, and no reliable method of communication, he'd stood every chance of ending up that way.

He'd been lucky to end up here.

He'd put this woman's life at risk.

He was helping her up the cliff now. He'd kicked his boots off in the water, which meant he was only wearing socks. The shale on the steep cliff was biting in, but that was the least of his worries. He'd been in the water for a couple of hours, trying to fight his way to shore, and he'd spent two days fighting the sea. He was freezing, and he was so tired all he wanted to do was sleep.

But the woman by his side was rigid with pain. She wasn't complaining, but when he'd put his arm around her waist and held her, supporting her as she walked, she hadn't pulled away. She wasn't big—five-four, five-five or so—and was slight with it. She had a smattering of freckles on her face, her chestnut curls clung wetly to her too-pale skin and her mouth was set in determination.

He just knew this woman didn't accept help unless there was a need.

'How far from the top of the cliff?' he asked, and she took a couple of deep breaths and managed to climb a few more feet before replying.

'Close. You want to go ahead? The back door's open.'

'Are you kidding?' His arm tightened around her. He was on her good side, aware that her left arm was useless and radiating pain. 'You're the lifesaver. Without you I'm a dead man.'

'Rocky will show you…where the pantry is…' She was talking in gasps. 'And the dog food. You'll survive.'

'I need *you* to show me where the pantry is. I think we're almost up now.'

'You'd know that how…?'

'I wouldn't,' he agreed humbly. 'I was just saying it to make you feel better.'

'Thank you,' she whispered.

'No, thank *you*,' he said, and held her tighter and put one foot after another and kept going.

And then they reached the top and he saw the house.

The island was a rocky outcrop, seeming almost to burst from the water in the midst of Bass Strait. He'd aimed for it simply because he'd had no choice—the boat had been taking on water and it had been the only land mass on the map—but from the sea it had seemed stark and inhospitable, with high cliffs looming out of the water. The small bay had seemed the only possible place to land, and even that had proved disastrous. What kind of a house could possibly be built *here*?

He reached the top of the cliff and saw a mansion.

Quite simply, it was extraordinary.

It was almost as if it was part of the island itself, long and low across the plateau, built of the same stone. In one sense it was an uncompromising fortress. In another sense it was pure fantasy.

Celtic columns faced the sea, supporting a vast pergola, with massive stone terraces underneath. Stone was stacked on stone, massive structures creating an impression of awe and wonder. There were sculptures everywhere—artworks built to withstand the elements. And the house itself… Huge French windows looked out over the sea. They were shuttered now, making the house look even more like a fortress. There was a vast swimming pool, carved to look like a natural rock pool. In this bleak weather it was covered by a solid mat.

He wouldn't be swimming for a while yet, he thought, but he looked at the house and thought he'd never seen anything more fantastic.

If he was being honest a one-room wooden hut would have looked good now, he conceded. But this…

'Safe,' he said, and the woman in his arms wilted a little. Her effort to climb the cliff had been huge.

'B… Back door…out of the wind,' she managed, and her voice was thready.

She'd fought to reach him in the water. She'd been injured trying to save him and now she'd managed to get up the cliff. He hadn't thought he had any strength left in him, but it was amazing what a body was capable of. His army instructors had told him that.

'No matter how dire, there's always another level of adrenalin. You'll never know it's there until you need it.'

He'd needed it once in a sticky situation in West Africa. He felt the woman slump beside him and needed it now. He stopped and turned her, and then swept her up into his arms.

She didn't protest. She was past protesting.

The little dog tore on ahead, showing him the way to the rear door, and in the end it was easy. Two minutes later he had her in the house and they were safe.

CHAPTER THREE

The first thing he had to do was get himself warm.

It seemed selfish, but he was so cold he couldn't function. And he needed to stay switched on for a while yet.

He laid his lifesaver on a vast settee in front of an open fire—miraculously it was lit, and the house was warm. She was back in her dry clothes and after her exertion on the cliff she wasn't shivering.

He was. His feet and hands were almost completely numb. He'd been in cold water for too long.

She knew it. She gripped his hand as he set her down and winced. 'Bathroom. Thataway,' she told him. 'You'll find clothes in the dressing room beside it.'

'I'll be fast.'

'Stay under water until you're warm,' she ordered, and now the urgent need had passed he knew she was right.

He'd been fighting to get his feet to work on the way up the cliff. He'd also been fighting to get his mind to think straight. Fuzzy images were playing at the edges and he had an almost overwhelming urge to lie by the fire and sleep.

He was trained to recognise hypothermia. He'd been starting to suffer in the water and the physical exertion hadn't been enough to raise his core temperature. He had to get himself warm if he was to be any use to this woman or to himself.

'You'll be okay? Don't move that arm.'

'As if I would. Go.'

So he went, and found a bathroom so sumptuous he might almost be in the palace at home. Any doubts as to how close he'd come to disaster were dispelled by the pain he felt when the warm water touched him.

There was a bench along the length of the shower. Two shower heads pointed hot water at him from different directions. He slumped on the bench and let the water do its work. Gradually the pain eased. He was battered and bruised, but he'd been more bruised than this after military exercises.

With his core heat back to normal he could almost think straight. Except he needed to sleep. He *really* needed to sleep.

There was a woman who needed him.

He towelled himself dry and moved to the next imperative. Clothes. This was a huge place. Who lived here?

The master bedroom was stunning, and whoever used it had a truly impressive wardrobe. There were over-the-top women's clothes—surely not belonging to the woman who'd saved him? He couldn't see her in flowing rainbow chiffon—but the guy's wardrobe was expansive, too. He found jogging pants that stretched to fit and the T-shirts were okay.

There were even socks and sheepskin slippers. And a cardigan just like his grandfather wore.

Exhaustion was still sweeping over him in waves, but at least his head was working. It had to keep working. He was dehydrated and starving and he needed to fix it. He found the kitchen, found a stack of long-life milk in the pantry and drank until the hollow, sick feeling in his stomach receded. Feeling absurdly pleased with himself, he headed back to the living room.

She was lying on her back, her eyes closed. He could see pain radiating out from her in waves.

'Hey,' he said, and she turned and managed a weak smile.

'Hey, yourself,' she managed. 'They look a whole lot better on you than Don.'

'Don?'

'Don and Marigold own this place.'

'Not you?'

'I wish.' She grimaced again. 'Actually, I *don't* wish. I've run out of good coffee.'

'You think it's time for introductions?' he asked, and she winced and tried for a smile.

'Claire. Claire Tremaine. I'm the island caretaker.'

'I'm Raoul,' he told her. 'Raoul de Castelaise.' Now surely wasn't the time for titles and formalities. 'Soldier. I'm pleased to meet you, Claire. In fact I can't begin to tell you *how* pleased. Tell me about your arm.'

'I guess…it's broken.'

'Can I see? I'll need to lift your windcheater.'

'I don't have a bra on.'

'So you don't. You want me to find you a bra?'

'I don't care,' she muttered. 'Look at my arm. Don't look at anything else.'

'No, ma'am.' He sat on the edge of the settee and helped her sit up, then carefully tugged off her windcheater. She only had her good arm in it, so it came off easily.

She'd ordered him not to look at anything else. That was a big ask.

Too big.

She was beautiful, he thought. She looked almost like an athlete, taut and lean. Her chestnut curls were wisping onto her naked shoulders.

She looked vulnerable and scared.

He headed back to the bathroom and brought out a towel, wrapping the fluffy whiteness around her so she was almost respectable but her arm was still exposed.

She hugged the towel to her as if she needed its comfort. The bravado she'd shown since the moment he'd met her in the water seemed to have disappeared.

She *was* scared?

Yeah. He was a big guy. Apart from the dog, she seemed to be in this house alone. She was semi-naked and injured.

Why *wouldn't* she be scared?

'Can I tell you that my grandmother thinks I'm

trustworthy?' he told her, tucking in the edges of the towel so it made an almost secure sarong. 'She tells the world what a good boy I am, and I'm not about to mess with her beliefs. I *am* trustworthy, Claire. I promise. If only because my grandmother's presence seems to spend a lot of time sitting on my shoulder. You're safe with me.'

And she managed a smile that was almost genuine.

'Scary Granny, huh.'

'You'd better believe it. But I can handle her.'

'And you love her?'

'You can believe that, too.'

And her smile softened, as if she really did believe him. As if somehow his words really had made her feel safe.

'Are you French?' she asked.

'I'm from Marétal. It's a small land-locked country near…'

'I know it,' she said, in an exclamation of surprise. 'Your army's taking part in the international army exercises in Tasmania. I looked it up.'

'You looked it up?'

'I get bored,' she admitted. Her voice was still tight, but she was making a huge effort to sound normal. 'I was listening to the Tasmanian news on the radio. They listed the countries taking part. I didn't know where Marétal was. So you're part of that exercise.' And then her voice grew tighter. 'Are there…are there any other soldiers lost overboard?'

'Only me—and it wasn't an army exercise,' he said ruefully. 'Despite the camouflage, I'm off duty. I took a friend's boat out from Hobart and got caught in the storm. I had two days being flung about Bass Strait, finally made it to the lee of your island and you know the rest. But my friend—the guy who owns *Rosebud*—is in Nepal. He doesn't know I took his boat and I didn't tell anyone I was going. It was a spur-of-the-moment decision. I broke all the rules and the army would agree that I've been an idiot.'

'You've paid the price.

'It could have been a whole lot higher.'

He was watching her arm while they talked. She was supporting it with her good hand, holding it slightly away from her body. Her shoulder looked odd. Squared off.

'Idiot or not, you might need to trust me with your arm,' he suggested. 'Can I touch it?'

'If you don't mind me screaming.'

'I'll be gentle,' he told her, and lightly ran his fingers down the front of her shoulder joint, thinking back to his first-aid courses. Thinking of anatomy.

'It feels dislocated,' he told her.

'It feels broken.'

'It probably feels worse than if it was broken.'

He put his fingers on her wrist and checked her pulse, then did it again at the elbow.

'You look like you know what you're doing,' she managed.

'I've been in the army for years. I'm a first-aider for my unit.

'You put on sticking plasters?'

'Sometimes it's more than that. When we're out of range of medical help this is what I do.'

'Like now?'

'I hope we're not out of range. You said you have a radio. Two-way? We must be within an hour's journey for a chopper coming from the mainland. Tell me where it is and I'll radio now.'

'Or not,' she said.

'Not?'

'No.' She winced. 'I know this sounds appalling… We have a radio—a big one. We also have back-up—a decent hand-held thing that's capable of sending signals to Hobart. But last time he was here Don—the owner—was messing around with it and dropped his beer into its workings. And the main radio seems to have been wiped out in the storm.'

'He dropped his beer…?'

'Yeah,' she said. 'If it had been Marigold it would have been a martini.' She closed her eyes. 'There's a first-aid kit in the kitchen,' she told him. 'I think I need it.'

'I doubt aspirin will help.'

'Marigold is allergic to pain. *Very* allergic. She's been known to demand morphine and a helicopter transfer to the mainland for a torn toenail. I'm thinking there'll be something decent in there.'

There was. He found enough painkillers to knock

out an elephant. Also muscle relaxant, and a dosage list that seemed to be made out for the Flying Doctor—Australia's remote medical service. The list didn't actually say *This much for a dislocated shoulder*, but he had enough experience to figure the dose. He made her hot, sweet tea—plus one for himself—then watched her take the pills he gave her.

'Stay still until that works,' he told her.

He found a blanket and covered her, and watched her curl into an almost foetal position on the settee. Rocky nestled on the floor by her side.

He tried to think of a plan.

Plans were thin on the ground and he was still having trouble thinking straight.

The drugs would ease her pain, he thought, but he also knew that the longer the shoulder stayed dislocated, the higher the chance of long-term damage.

In the Middle East he'd had a mate who had…

Um, no. He wasn't going there.

He did a further tour and found the radio in a truly impressive study. Claire had been right: there was no transmission. He headed outside and saw a wooden building blasted to splinters. A huge radio antenna lay smashed among the timber.

No joy there.

'You're on your own,' he muttered, and pushed away the waves of exhaustion and headed back to the living room.

She was still lying where he'd left her, but her rigidity seemed to have lessened.

He knelt beside her. 'Better?'

'Better,' she whispered. 'Just leave me be.'

'I can't do that. Claire, we're going to have to get that arm back into position.'

'My arm wants to stay really still.'

'And I'm going to have to hurt you,' he told her. 'But if I don't hurt you now you may have long-term damage.'

'How do I know it's not broken?'

'You don't. I don't. So I'm using basic first aid, and the first rule is *Do no harm*. We were taught a method which only sometimes works, but its huge advantage is that it won't hurt a fracture. If there's a fracture the arm will scream at you and you'll scream at me and we'll stop.' He hoped. 'Claire, I need you to lie on your front and let your arm hang down. We'll put a few cushions under you so your arm is high enough to hang freely. Then I'm going to gradually weight your arm, using sticking plaster to attach things like cans of beans...'

'Beans?'

'Anything I can find.' He smiled. 'In an emergency, anything goes. My first-aid trainer said if I ask you to grip the cans then your arm will tense, so I just need to stick them on you as dead weights. Then we'll let the nice drugs do their work. You'll lie back and think of England, and the tins of beans will tug your arm down, and if you relax completely then I'm hoping it'll pop back in.'

'Think of England?'

'Or sunbeams,' he told her. 'Anything to take your mind off your arm.'

She appeared to think about that for a moment, maybe choosing from a list of options. And then she opened her eyes and glanced up at him, taking in his appearance. From head to toe.

'Nice,' she whispered. 'I think I'll think about *you*. If you knew how different you look to Don... Don fills his T-shirt up with beer belly. You fill it up with...you.'

'Me?'

'Muscles.'

Right. It was the drugs talking, he thought. He needed to stop looking into her eyes and quit smiling at her like an idiot and think of her as a patient. As one of the guys in his unit, injured in the field. *Work.*

Nothing personal at all.

But he needed to get her relaxed. He knelt beside her and pushed a damp curl from her eyes. She was little and dark and feisty, and her freckles were very, very cute. Her hair was still damp from her soaking. He would have liked to get her completely dry, but he was working through a list of imperatives. Arm first.

'H... How does this work?' she muttered.

'The socket's like a cup,' he told her. 'I think your arm's slipped out of the cup, but it still has muscles that want it to go back in. If we weight it, and you're relaxed, then your muscles have a chance to pull it back into place.'

That was the theory, anyway. *If* it worked. *If* the arm wasn't broken. But the weighting method was the only safe course of action. To pull on a broken arm could mean disaster. Gradual weighting was the only way, but she had to trust him.

And it seemed she did.

'Do it,' she said, and smiled up at him. 'Only we don't have baked beans. How about tins of caviar?'

'You're kidding?'

'No. But there are tinned tomatoes as well.' Then she appeared to brighten. 'And we have tins of truly appalling instant coffee. It'd be great if they could be useful for something.'

She smiled up at him and he thought of the pain she was suffering, and the sheer courage she was showing, and the fact that she was smiling to make *him* smile...

And he smiled back at her and backed away— because a man had to back away fast from a smile like that—and went to find some truly useful cans of coffee.

Somehow he stayed businesslike. Professional. Somehow he followed the instructions in his head from first-aid training in the field. He taped on the weights. He watched for her to react from too much pain, but although she winced as he weighted her arm she didn't make a murmur.

He put on as much weight as he thought she could tolerate and then he sat beside her and waited.

'What do we do now?' she asked.

'Relax. Forget the arm. Tell you what,' he said. 'I'll tell you a story.'

'What sort of story?'

He thought about it. He needed a story that would make her almost soporific so the arm would totally relax.

'How about *Goldilocks and the Three Bears*?' he suggested, and she choked.

'Really?'

'Has anyone ever read it to you?'

'I guess…not for a very long time.'

'Same for me,' he told her. 'So correct me if I get the bears muddled. Okay, here goes.'

And he sat by the couch and stroked her hair and told her the story of the three bears. It was a simple story—not long enough—so he had to embellish it. He had Goldilocks as a modern-day Bond girl, escaping from villains. He had his bears trying to figure the villains from the good guys, and he put in a bit of drama for good measure.

In other words he had fun, blocking the fuzziness in his own head with the need to keep her attention. And as Baby Bear found Goldilocks, and good guys and baddies were sorted, and baddies were dispatched with buckets of Mama Bear's too-hot porridge, and they all settled down for toast and marmalade, Claire's arm did what he'd desperately hoped it would do. It clicked back into its socket.

In the silence of the room, between breaks in the very exciting narrative, they actually heard it pop.

The relief did his head in.

It was almost as if he hadn't realised what stress he'd been under until the arm clicked back into place. The sound was like an off switch, clicking in his brain.

For the first time in his life he felt as if he was going to faint. He put his head between his knees—because it was either that or keel over. And Claire's fingers touched his hair, running through the still damp strands. Caressing.

'It's done,' she whispered. 'Thank you.'

'Thank *you*,' he managed. 'I couldn't have borne it if you'd suffered permanent damage saving me. Claire, I need to fix you a sling.'

'Raoul... First... Lie here,' she whispered. 'Please... Just...hold me.'

He'd been in deadly peril for two days. For a few hours earlier today he'd been sure he'd drown.

He was past exhaustion. He was past anything. Maybe Claire knew it. Maybe Claire felt the same.

'Sling first,' he muttered, and managed to tie her arm so it wouldn't slip, but then he was done.

'I need to sleep,' Claire murmured. 'The drugs... My arm... It's all okay, but... Raoul, stay with me.'

She was lying on the huge settee, tousled, part-wrapped in a fleecy towel, part-covered by the huge blanket he'd found. The fire was putting out a gentle warmth.

He fought for sense but he was losing. He managed to toss more logs on the fire and then he stared into the flames thinking...*nothing*. Goldilocks and the three bears seemed very far away. Everything seemed very far away.

But Claire was edging sideways to give him room to lie with her.

There was no choice. He sat down on the settee and she put her hand up and touched his face.

'We're safe,' she whispered. 'Nice. Stay.'

He lay down, but the sofa wasn't big enough to avoid touching. And it seemed the most natural thing in the world that he put his arms around her.

She curled into him with a sleepy murmur.

'Nice,' she said again. 'Sleep.'

He woke and it was still daylight. Was it late afternoon or was it the next day? For now he didn't know and didn't care.

He was still on the settee. The room was warm. *He* was warm. The fire was a mass of glowing embers.

He was holding Claire.

There were aches in his body, just waiting to make themselves known. He could feel them lurking. They'd make themselves known if he moved.

But for now he had no intention of moving. He lay with the warmth of the woman beside him: a gentle, amazing comfort. Her towel had slipped. He was lying on her uninjured side. Her naked body was against his chest and he was cradling her to him. She was using his chest as a pillow.

He had a T-shirt on but it didn't feel like it. Her warmth made it feel as if she was almost a part of him.

He could feel her heartbeat. Her hair had dried and was tumbling across his chest, and her breathing was deep and even.

After the perils, the fear, the exhaustion of the last two days, he was filled with a sense of peace so great it threatened to overwhelm him.

He'd been in dangerous situations before. He'd had moments when he'd ended up sleeping tight with other members of his unit, some of them women. He'd held people when they'd been in mutual danger.

But he'd never felt like this, he thought. As if this woman was *right*.

As if this woman was part of him.

That was a crazy thought, he decided, and he hadn't even taken any drugs. What was going on?

He must have moved a little, because Claire stirred and opened her eyes and shifted a fraction. She didn't move far, though. She was still cradled against him.

Her heartbeat was still his.

'Nice,' she said, as she'd said before she'd slept, and it was like a blessing.

'Nice?'

'The wind's died.'

It had, too. He hadn't noticed.

He had sensory overload.He couldn't get past the feeling of the woman in his arms.

'Pain?' he asked, and she seemed to think about it.

'Nope,' she said at last. 'Not if I lie really still.'

That suited him. They lay really still. Rocky was snuffling under the settee. Maybe that was what had woken them.

Or other, more mundane things.

'I need the bathroom,' she murmured, and he conceded that he did, too. And the fire needed more logs. And, to tell the truth, he was so hungry he could eat a horse—the milk and tea had barely hit the sides—but he was prepared to ignore everything if she'd stay where she was. But now Rocky had his paws up on the settee and was looking at them with bright, expectant eyes.

'That's his "feed me" look,' Claire murmured, and she moved a little so she could scratch behind his ear with her good hand. And then she said, in a different voice, 'I've lost my towel.'

'So you have.' It was hard not to sound complacent.

She tugged back, hauled the blanket up across her breasts and tried a glare. It wasn't a very big glare. Those drugs must have packed a fair punch, he thought. She still looked dazed.

Actually...*beautifully* dazed. She had wide green eyes that seemed to be struggling to focus. She had skin that seemed almost translucent. Her lashes were long and curled a little, and her nose was ever so slightly snubbed.

'You noticed,' she said accusingly, and he shook his head.

'No, ma'am. I've been looking at Rocky all the time.'

'Liar.'

'Yes, ma'am.'

She grinned, and he thought that if she'd had two good hands she might have punched him. But one was still pretty much tied up. He was safe.

'Life,' she said.

'Sorry?'

'We fought to keep it. We might as well get on with it.'

'You mean we need to feed the fire, go to the bathroom, feed the dog, find something to eat ourselves...'

'And think of some way to contact the mainland.' Her smile faded. 'Will people be looking for you?'

He thought of his minders. At midday, when he'd spoken to Franz, he had been supposed to be with his unit. His minders had therefore been off duty. At six that night they'd have rung to check his itinerary for the following day.

He'd have been expected to be back well before six. They'd have rung and someone would have told them he was off duty. Then they'd have contacted Franz. 'He's off duty as of this morning. I believe he's planning on returning home,' he would have told them, and then someone would have been sent to check his kit and discovered it was still where it was supposed to be.

It would have taken his minders about thirty seconds after that to panic.

'What is it?' she said, and pushed herself up, wincing a bit as she moved her arm.

'What?'

'Your face. Someone's looking for you right now. Someone's terrified. Your wife? Partner? Family?'

'I don't have a wife or partner.'

'Family? Parents?'

'My parents died when I was five, but I do have grandparents.'

'Back in Marétal?'

'Yes.' He closed his eyes, thinking of the fuss when his grandparents discovered he was missing. Then he thought of how long he'd been gone. After all this time it wouldn't be fuss. It would be horror. 'I imagine they'll know I'm missing.'

She was sitting up now, blanket tucked to her chin, concentrating on the problem at hand. 'Don't worry too much,' she told him. 'The wind's died. I suspect you'll be mortified, but the Australian Air Sea Rescue services are good. They can probably track the wind and the currents and get a fair idea of your direction. If I was them I'd be checking the islands first. There's only about ten. Any minute now we'll have choppers overhead, searching for one lost soldier.'

He felt sick.

'Don't worry,' Claire said again. 'I imagine it's embarrassing, getting rescued twice, once even by a girl, but you'll just have to cop it.'

'I won't,' he told her.

'Are you going to tell me how you can avoid it?'

'I already *have* avoided it,' he said, goaded. 'I didn't tell anyone I was going sailing. What's more, I took my friend's boat. My friend's currently trying to climb Annapurna Two in Nepal. He won't know I'm missing and he won't know his boat's missing. No one knows I went to sea. I could be anywhere and my...my grandparents will be devastated.'

His grandparents?

This wasn't just about his grandparents, he thought. His bodyguard consisted of two skilled, decent men who'd feel as if they'd failed. The top brass of the army would be mortified. His friends would be appalled. And, back home, the media would be in a feeding frenzy. *Heir to the Throne Disappears!* It didn't bear thinking about.

He would have groaned if it would do any good.

It wouldn't.

'Raoul...'

'Mmm?'

'We all do dumb things,' she told him, and put her good hand on his knee. 'Some dumber than others.

But, hey, you've lived to be embarrassed. The supply boat's due next Monday. You'll climb aboard, they'll let everyone know, and by the time you reach Hobart the fuss will have died down. You might need to apologise to a few people and go home and hug your grandparents, but it's no big deal. So one soldier's gone AWOL? If they don't think you've drowned then they'll probably assume you're in a bar somewhere. Or with a woman.'

And then she had the temerity to grin.

'Actually, they're both true. You're very much with a woman, and if you go through that door there's a truly excellent bar.'

'I think I need it,' he said, and she chuckled and tried to stand.

She wobbled a bit and he rose to steady her.

'What did you give me?' she demanded. 'I feel like I've had enough drugs to down an elephant.'

'Or to not scream when your arm went back in. You were very brave.'

'I was, wasn't I?' she said smugly. 'So I'm brave and you're lost. And my arm's back to where it belongs. They're the givens. For the rest...we just have to get on with it.'

'I really can't get off this place until next Monday?'

'We can try and fix the transmitter,' she told him. 'Are you any good with electronics?'

'No.'

'Then I'm vetoing that as a plan straight away,'

she told him. 'I have no intention of saving you twice. Now, Raoul…?'

'Yes?'

'Put some logs on the fire while I feed Rocky. We have life to get on with.'

'Yes, ma'am,' he said, because there was nothing else to say. Nothing at all.

CHAPTER FOUR

THIS MORNING SHE'D been bored.

This morning her entire desire in life had been a decent cup of coffee.

She was not bored now, and her desire was taking a new and entirely inappropriate direction.

Maybe she should be nervous. This guy was seriously big. He had the brawn and build of a well-honed military machine. Even washed up on the beach he'd looked awesome.

She stood under the shower and let the hot water run over her battered body as she let her mind drift where it willed.

It willed straight to Raoul.

She was alone on this island with a guy she didn't know. A seriously big guy. A seriously good-looking guy. He was dark-haired and tanned and his grey eyes were creased at the edges. Was the weathering on his face from years of military exercises in tough conditions? She wasn't sure if she was right, but she guessed she was.

He was kind. He was also skilled. He'd managed to get her arm back into place and the relief had been enormous. He was also worried about his grandparents. She could see that. One lone soldier AWOL from the army wouldn't cause a fuss, but she'd seen that he was distressed. Of course the army would contact his family, and of course it distressed Raoul that his grandparents would worry. Because he was…a good guy.

Raoul. Nice name, she thought. Nice guy. And a seriously sexy accent. Almost French, with something else in the mix.

Sexy.

And there lay the rub. There lay the reason why she should stop thinking about Raoul right now.

'Are you okay in there?'

His voice almost made her jump out of her skin and when she landed she had to fight to get her voice in order.

'F… Fine.'

'Dinner's ready when you are. I already ate, but I'm ready to eat again.'

'You already *ate*?'

'Your refrigerator's amazing. Or should I say refrigerators, plural. Wow. I opened one to check and three eggs almost fell into my hand. So I ate them. You do realise eating's been low on my priority list over the last few days? Having had my pre-dinner boiled egg snack, I'm now serious about making dinner proper. But first I'm here to towel my lady's back, if she wants it towelled, because it's occurred to me that one-arm towelling might be hard.'

There were things there for a woman to consider. A lot of things. She was alone on the island with this guy. Every sensible part of her said she shouldn't accept his help.

Raoul had put a plastic outdoor chair in the shower before he'd let her into the bathroom. He'd fussed, but she'd assured him she was okay. She'd been able to kick off her salty clothes herself, and sitting under the hot water had been easy. She'd even managed to shampoo her hair with one hand.

But now… The wussy part of her said she didn't know how she *could* towel herself with one arm, especially as the painkillers were still making her feel a bit fuzzy. And there was a tiny part of her—a really dangerous part—that was saying she wouldn't mind being towelled by this guy.

She was twenty-eight years old. She was hardly a prude. He was…

Yeah, enough.

But she had three voices in her head now. One saying, *Safe*, one saying, *Sensible*, the other saying, *Yes!*

She had an internal vote and *Safe* and *Sensible* were outvoted by about a hundred to two.

'Yes,' she whispered, but he didn't hear.

'Claire? Are you okay?'

'I'm fine,' she said. 'And, yes, please—I think I *do* need help to get dry.'

It wasn't a bad feeling.

Okay, it was an incredible feeling. He had his

hands full of lush white towel and he was carefully towelling Claire Tremaine dry.

She was beautiful. Every inch of her was beautiful. She'd emerged naked from the shower. She'd stood with rivulets of warm water streaming down her body and he'd never seen anything more beautiful in his life.

If he hadn't spent the last two days having cold shower after cold shower, he might have seriously thought of taking one now. Instead of which he had to get his thoughts under control and do what he was here for—get the lady dry.

She'd grabbed a towel, too, but with only one good hand she could do little. She dried her face and rubbed her front, which was okay because that meant he didn't have to dry her breasts. Which would have been hard. But he did have to towel her hair. He did have to run the towel down the smooth contours of her back. He did need to stoop to dry her gorgeous legs.

She was a small woman, but her legs seemed to go on forever. How did *that* happen?

She was gorgeous.

When he'd knocked on the bathroom door he'd just put steak in the microwave to defrost and until he'd entered the bathroom that steak had been pretty much uppermost in his thoughts.

Not now. The steak could turn into dust for all he cared. Every sense was tuned to this woman.

Every part of his body...

'I think I'm dry,' she said, in a voice that was shaky, but not shaky in a pained kind of way. It was shaky in a way that told him she was as aware of him as he was of her.

He could gather her up right now...

Yeah, like *that* could happen. This woman had hauled him out of the water and let him into her home. She'd been injured on his behalf. She was still slightly drug-affected. No, make that a *lot* drug-affected. He'd given her more painkillers before she'd gone to shower.

Hitting on her now would be all sorts of wrong.

But she was looking at him with huge eyes, slightly dazed, and her fingers were touching his hair as he stooped to dry her legs.

'Raoul...' she whispered, and he rose and stepped away fast.

'Yeah. You're done,' he told her. 'Where can I find you some clothes? Something sensible.'

He spoke too loud, too emphatically, and the emphasis on the last word was like a slap to them both. *Sensible.* That was the way to go.

'I... My bedroom... It's right next door. There's a jogging suit in the third drawer of the dresser. Knickers in the top drawer. I'm ditching the idea of a bra. But I can get them.'

'Stay where you are,' he said roughly, and backed away fast.

Because it might be sensible to help her into the bedroom and help her get dressed, but there was a bed in the bedroom, and a man had limits, and his were already stretched close to breaking.

So he headed into the bedroom and found the jogging suit, and then he opened the knicker drawer and had to take a deep breath before he felt sensible again. He picked up the first pair of knickers that came to hand and practically slammed the drawer shut. A pair of sheepskin bootees stood beside the bed. Excellent. They weren't sexy in the least.

He headed back to the bathroom, thought about helping her, then decided it might be hard but she should be able to cope herself and it would be far, far safer if he stayed on his side of the door.

He knocked and slipped the clothes around the door, without opening it wide enough for him to see her. They needed barriers, he thought. Big barriers. Preferably barriers with locks on them.

He stepped away from the door as if it was red-hot.

'Steak in ten minutes,' he said. 'If you're up to it. If the painkillers aren't making you too dizzy?'

'The painkillers aren't making me too dizzy,' she told him, and then she stopped.

And he thought he knew what she was about to say because he was feeling the same.

The *painkillers* weren't making her dizzy, but something else was.

The same something that was doing his head in?

* * *

She dressed, and replaced the basic sling Raoul had fashioned for her.

Her arm was still painful, but it was a steady, bruised ache, not the searing pain she'd experienced when it was dislocated.

She was dry, she was warm, and she was dressed. She hauled a comb through her curls and thought she looked almost presentable. Almost respectable. *Yeah*. She looked at herself in the mirror. Her jogging suit was baggy and old. She had on her huge sheepskin boots. Her hair was combed but still damp and she didn't have the energy to dry it. There was no way she had the energy for makeup, either.

'It's take me as I am,' she said out loud, and then winced.

Take me?

What was she thinking?

Rocky was sitting at her feet. He looked up at her quizzically, as if guessing her thoughts, and she gave him a rueful smile.

'You and I have been alone too long,' she told him. 'Four months and one lone guy enters our world...'

One *gorgeous* guy. A guy with an accent to make a girl's toes curl. A guy who was gentle and kind. A guy who'd lost his parents, who knew what being alone felt like.

A kindred spirit?

'Yeah, those drugs are really doing something to you,' she muttered, and adjusted her sling a bit— not because she needed to, but because adjusting it caused her arm to twinge and she felt she needed a little bit of pain right now.

Pain equalled reality. Reality was good.

Reality was getting this guy off her island and going back to her stint of self-imposed exile.

She could smell steak. And onions. Raoul was cooking for her.

'It needed only that,' she muttered, and took a last moment to try and grasp at a reality that was looking more and more elusive.

And then she went to find Raoul.

'Hey.' Raoul turned as she entered the kitchen.

He smiled at her, his eyes raking her from her toes to the top of her head, and his smile said he approved. Of the saggy jogging suit. Of everything. That smile was enough to do a girl's head in.

'Well done. Feel better?'

'I…yes.' Of course she did. A thousand times better. She was clean and she was warm and she was about to be fed. What else could a woman want?

Who else?

'I feel great,' she said, a bit too heartily, and then blinked as he tugged a chair out for her. All this and manners, too?

'You don't need to do this,' she told him. 'I'm the servant here, remember?'

'The servant?'

'Don and Marigold own the island, but they never come here in winter. They needed a caretaker. Rocky and I applied for the job.'

'Just Rocky and you?' He turned to flip the steaks. 'That's hardly safe.'

'There's also supposed to be a handyman-cum-gardener. What they didn't tell me was that he'd quit. He left on the boat I arrived on, and Don and Marigold headed to Europe without finding a replacement.'

He was organising chips on plates. *Chips!* Yeah, they were the frozen oven variety, but she totally approved. Steak and chips and onions. And baby peas, and slivered carrots sautéed in butter. *Wow,* she thought. *Turn back the rescue boats. I'm keeping him.*

Um…*not.*

Drugs, she reminded herself. She really had had a lot of them.

'Don and Marigold need to wake up,' he told her, organising the plates to his satisfaction.

He flipped the steak and veggies on, then carried them to the table, sitting down before her as if this was something they did every day of the week. Then he looked at her sling and leaned over and chopped up her steak. The sensation of being cared for was almost indescribable.

Yeah, maybe she was bordering on delusional…

'They're breaking every rule in the Occupational Safety Code,' he told her, sitting back down again and turning his attention to his own meal. 'Leaving someone in such isolation. Or don't they have those rules in Australia?'

'They do.'

'So why are you still on the island? Come to think about it, why were you here in the first place?'

She didn't answer for a while. She didn't need to. The steak was excellent, as were the accompaniments. She hadn't eaten since breakfast and she'd had a swim and a shock. She could be excused for making food her priority.

But the question hung. *'Why were you here in the first place?'*

It wasn't his business, she thought. But a tiny voice in the back of her mind said, *Why not tell him? Why not say it like it is?*

She hadn't told anyone. She'd simply fled.

'I've been accused of fraud,' she said.

He said nothing.

So what had she expected? Fireworks? Shock? Horror? At least a token of dismay? Instead he concentrated on his second piece of steak as if it was the most important thing in the world. And, because there was nothing else to do, she focused on her food, too. She ate a few more chips and her world settled a little and she felt better.

Lighter.

It was as if the elephant was in the room, but at least it was no longer inside her.

'It couldn't have been a very big fraud,' he said

at last, eying the near empty bowl of chips with due consideration.

'What? Why?'

'You're not in jail and you've taken a job as a caretaker in one of the most inhospitable places on the earth. This might be a great house, but you're not living in luxury. So it was either a very small fraud or you've cleverly stacked what you've defrauded away so you can be a billionaire in your old age.'

'I could have paid it back.'

'I suspect if you'd paid it back you wouldn't be on this island. Do you want to tell me about it?'

No, she thought. And then she thought, *Okay, the elephant's out*. But it was still a very big elephant. Regardless of how trivial this guy made it sound.

'It was big,' she told him. 'Something like seven million Australian dollars.'

He shook his head in disbelief. 'Ma'am, if you're hiding that kind of cash you shouldn't let strange men rifle through your knicker drawer.'

And she chuckled. She couldn't help herself.

She laughed, and then she thought, *That's the first time I've laughed since...since...*

She couldn't remember.

'I didn't do it,' she said, and her desire to laugh died. Her thoughts went back to that last day, standing in her boss's office, white with shock. *I didn't do it.*

He hadn't believed her. Why would he?

'So?' Raoul said encouragingly. 'I believe you. You didn't do it, so...the butler?'

She choked again, and he smiled and took another chip and handed it across the table to her.

She took it and ate it, and he kept smiling at her, and his smile was doing something to her insides...

'That's it,' he told her. 'Nice, greasy carbohydrates. Best thing in the world for trauma. Like telling me all about the butler. Jam doughnuts would be better, but for now we're stuck with chips. If not the butler, who?'

'Felicity,' she whispered, and he nodded.

'Of course. I should have guessed. I was lacking a few clues, though. So tell me about Felicity.'

'She's perfect.'

'You mean she probably has the seven million?'

'I guess.'

'Yep, she's perfect, then. Pretty, too, I'll bet.'

And Claire thought of pretty, perfect Felicity and found it hard not to start shaking. But suddenly Raoul's hand was over hers—big, comforting, warm. Joking was put aside.

'Tell me,' he said, and so she did.

From the beginning. All of it.

Of the tiny town where she was raised, of her single mum, of being treated like trash. Of her mum's death when she was fifteen. Of the scholarship and her determination to get out. Of law school and commerce, a double degree. Of academic brilliance and sheer hard work.

Once she'd graduated she'd taken a job in Legal Assistance. It had been a great organisation—helping the underprivileged with legal advice and representation when they couldn't afford it. She'd enjoyed it. Then she'd won a huge legal case that had received national headlines, and she'd been headhunted by one of the most prestigious law firms in Australia. She had been stupid enough to accept.

Only she hadn't been *one of them*.

'I was the odd one out,' she told him. 'An experiment. They select their lawyers on the basis of family and connections, but one of the senior partners had the noble idea that they should try something else—hire someone on merit. They broke their rules when they hired me. Three others were hired at the same time, on the old system. They'd gone to the same school and the same universities. They were the best of friends. But there was a fourth, and because of me he missed out on a job. So they hated me from day one. I tried not to care. I put my head down and worked. But the more I got ahead the more they hated me.'

'And then?'

'Then there was a problem,' she said, talking almost to herself. 'Insider trading, they call it. Someone in the firm knew something and passed the information on. There was a deal. Someone outside the company made seven million dollars and the media started asking questions. The company had to point the finger at someone.'

'Was there evidence?'

'Of course there was evidence,' she told him. 'A paper trail leading straight back to me. So I was called into the office of the managing director. I had a choice, he said. I could resign and the company's insurer would repay costs, cover the fiasco and keep the company's name clean and out of the courts. Or I could go to jail.' She shrugged. 'They had the best legal team in Australia covering their backs and I was a nobody. I *had* nobody. It didn't seem like much of a choice.'

'But if it wasn't you…?'

She sighed. 'A week after I left Felicity left. For Paris. I have no proof of anything, but Felicity's partner just happens to be the nephew of the managing director, and Felicity had the desk next to mine. So here I am. I haven't been charged with anything, but the legal fraternity in Australia is tight. My time as a corporate lawyer is over. I might be able to get back into Legal Assistance, but even there I'm now tainted. I took this job to take some time and think through my options, but I don't have many.'

'You could sue,' he said. 'You could fight.'

'Yeah?' She shrugged, and then gave a rueful smile. 'Maybe I could,' she said. 'But it'd cost a fortune. I'd risk debt, or worse, and I'd also risk…'

'Risk what?'

'Attention,' she whispered. 'The media would be all over it. Ever since I was a kid I knew to keep my head down. To stay unnoticed. It's always been safest.' She took a deep breath. 'When I left to go to university our local publican said, "You'll be back, girl. A girl like you…raised in the gutter… you've got airs if you think you'll ever get rid of the stink." But I gave myself airs and this is where it's left me.'

'I wish you'd punched him.'

And the thought suddenly cheered her. She thought back to the smirking publican and wished, quite fiercely, that she'd had the skills then that she had now.

'I could have,' she said, attempting to lighten her voice. 'I have a black belt in karate. I may like keeping myself to myself, but physically if you mess with me you're in trouble. Even if I'm one-handed.'

He looked at her in astonishment. 'You're kidding?'

'Like the publican said, you can take the girl out of the gutter, but you can never take the gutter out of the girl. I learned karate, and the gym I went to taught me base moves as well. I can fight clean or I can fight dirty.'

'That sounds like a warning.'

She grinned. 'If you like. Rocky knows to treat me with respect.' Her smile faded. 'But respect for me is a bit thin on the ground. Bob Maker was a bully and a drunk, but he did get one thing right. Trying to move away from my roots was a mistake. I'll never try it again.'

'So you won't fight? You'll calmly go back where you came from?'

She smiled again at that, but ruefully. 'I wouldn't fit,' she said. 'Legal Assistance is my first love. It's a fantastic organisation. They helped me when Mum died and I was trying to prove I could live independently, but I'm not sure I can go back there. That's what this is all about. Rocky and I are taking six months to think about it. So what about you?'

'What do you mean?'

'Meaning you don't have a mum and dad. I assume your grandparents raised you? Was joining the army a big step?'

He thought about it for a moment. For a long moment. She'd told him so much about herself. It was only fair to explain his background.

But a part of him…*couldn't*. She was sitting opposite him with total trust. She was relaxed, eating her chips, smiling, and she'd just explained how social class had destroyed her career.

Over the years Raoul had watched the almost grotesque change in people's attitudes when his royal title was revealed. Sometimes people fawned. Sometimes people backed away.

With her background, with her recent hurt and with her desire to stay in the background, he suspected Claire would back away fast, and he didn't want that. An urgent voice in his head was starting to say, *This is important. Give it time. Get to know her on equal terms.*

Had his joining the army been a big step?

'I guess it was,' he said at last. 'I'm an officer. I had to fight to get where I was, and to be accepted.'

And wasn't that the truth? Of course he'd been seen as different. It had taken him years to break down barriers, and every now and then the barriers would rise back up.

Like now. If a normal soldier went AWOL questions would be asked, but unless there was a suggestion of foul play the army usually adopted a policy of wait and see. After weeks of tough field exercise some men got drunk, found women, got themselves into places that took them a while to get out of. No one would put out an international alert on *their* disappearance.

Whereas for him…

He had no doubts about the scale of the hue and cry that would be happening. *Heir to the throne of Marétal disappears.* He closed his eyes, thinking of the distress. The fuss. He'd been so stupid.

'You're still tired,' Claire told him, and he thought about explaining and decided again that he didn't want to. Not yet.

He *was* tired. 'I guess…'

'Let's both sleep,' she told him. 'Leave the dishes. They'll wait until morning. I'm beat.'

'The drugs will still be making you dozy.'

'And being tossed around in a bathtub for two days and almost drowned will be making *you* dozy,' she told him. She rose and took a glass of water.

'Pick a bedroom. Any bedroom but mine. Marigold leaves toiletries for her guests—there'll be razors and toothbrushes…everything you need. Raoul, thank you for the meal. Thank you for everything. I'm going to bed.'

She headed for the door. He watched her go. Then… 'Claire?'

She paused and looked back at him. 'Yes?'

'Thank you,' he said softly. 'Thank you for saving my life and thank you…for just being you. And if I ever meet the appalling Felicity it'll be more than karate that comes into play. It would be my privilege to fight for you.'

She smiled, but absently. 'Thank you, but don't get your hopes up,' she told him. 'It's money and power that keeps the Felicitys of this world out of trouble, and neither of us have even close to what *they* have. But there are compensations. That was an awesome steak.'

And then she raised her glass, as if in a toast.

'Here's to what we *do* have,' she told him. 'And here's to never aspiring to more.' She gave a rueful smile and turned and disappeared.

He didn't follow. Yes, he'd been battered, but he had already slept and there was no way he could sleep now.

He washed the dishes, because that was what you did. Once upon a time he hadn't known what a dish-cloth was, but years of roughing it in army camps had knocked that out of him.

Then he figured he should check the damage to the radio transmitter. He'd look pretty stupid if it was just a case of the antenna falling over. And he also needed something to occupy his mind that wasn't Claire.

That was a hard ask. She'd gone to bed, but in a way she was still with him.

She'd told a stark tale and it had hurt her to tell it. He'd been able to tell by the way her face had set as she'd told it. By the way she'd laughed afterwards. He had just been able to...*tell*.

She was right under his skin.

He wanted to find the unknown Felicity and send her to the gutter in Claire's place. He wanted to ruin the entire firm she'd worked for.

He could. Maybe he would.

He thought of what he had—the resources, the power—and thought he should tell her.

Why? What good would it possibly do for Claire to know now what power he could wield?

She was treating him as a companion. He had no doubt that her dreadful little story wouldn't have been told if he'd first appeared to her in royal regalia. But he'd been in army gear, and she'd have had no way of recognising the discreet crown emblazoned on the sleeve. To her he was just a soldier—someone who'd come up through the ranks. A kid with no parents.

She thought he was the same as she was, and he

didn't mind her thinking it. No, he *wanted* her to think it.

Why? Tired as he was, the warning bells that seemed to have been installed in his brain since his parents' death were suddenly jangling. He'd been a loner since then—or maybe even earlier. The royal household was always full of people, but whenever he needed comfort he never knew who it was who'd do the comforting. Whose job it was that week…

He'd learned not to need comfort. People came and went. He didn't get attached.

Why was he suddenly thinking of this in relation to Claire?

He shook his head, trying to rid himself of thoughts that were jumbling. He was overtired, he thought, still battered, still not thinking straight. He needed to be practical.

First things first. He didn't intend to spend the rest of his time here wearing Don's clothes. He found the laundry and put his and Claire's salt-laden clothes in the washing machine.

But that was weirdly intimate, too. He shoved them in without looking at them, but as he closed the machine door and the clothes started to tumble he saw Claire's wispy bra tangling with his army gear.

Maybe he should have hand-washed it, he thought, but then again…maybe not.

He turned his back on the laundry, thinking as he

did that it was over the top—a vast wet room with every machine a laundry could ever hold.

How was it all powered? There was no mains power here, and if there had been it would have surely been knocked out by the storm.

He did a quick reconnaissance of the house, avoiding the passage to Claire's self-contained apartment. Claire's apartment was sparsely furnished, but the rest of the house not so much. Every room was enormous. Every room was lavish. He had a choice of bedrooms, all made up and ready. The unknown Don and Marigold might obviously sweep in at a moment's notice with a bevy of guests.

The refrigerators would cope.

But the power…?

He ended up in the basement and found his answer. Here was a vast bank of batteries, presumably linked to solar panels. This explained why the house was still warm, the refrigerators still operating.

It still wasn't safe for Claire to be here, he thought. Not alone.

Which led to figuring out the radio. He'd found the second transmitter in the study. It was huge and it was useless.

Frustrated, he found a torch and ventured outside. The wind was still up, catching him in its icy chill, but he'd been in conditions far worse than this during his service. The antenna had been attached to one of the outbuildings and it had crashed down during the storm. It lay smashed across the rocks, and with it lay the remains of a satellite dish.

This had been some communications system. A much smaller one would have been far less prone to damage.

Someone had wanted the best—so they could tune into a football game in Outer Mongolia if they wished. He stared bitterly at the over-the-top equipment and thought they could even have used this to talk to Mars if there had been anyone on Mars to hear.

But not now. A small radio might have been within his power to fix. This, he hadn't a hope of fixing.

In this day and age surely there must be *some* method of communicating with the mainland.

Smoke signals?

Right.

He'd seen the maps. This island was far away from normal shipping channels. There might be the odd fishing trawler around, but after the storm the sea would be churned for days. Fishing fleets would stay in port until things settled.

He thought of his grandparents and felt ill.

There was nothing he could do about their distress. *Nothing.*

He could go to bed and worry about it there.

He did go to bed—in the smallest of the over-the-top bedrooms. He lay in the dark and decided that worrying achieved nothing. He should turn his mind off tomorrow and simply appreciate that he was in a warm bed, his world had stopped rocking and he was safe.

He did manage to turn his mind off worrying.

He didn't quite succeed in turning his mind off Claire.

CHAPTER FIVE

SHE WOKE AND the sun was streaming into her little bedroom. She was safe in her own bed, Rocky was asleep on her feet—and she was sore.

Very sore. She shifted a little and her arm protested in no uncertain terms.

She opened her eyes and saw a note propped against a glass of water.

Pills, it said. *Pain. When you wake take these. Don't try and move until they take effect.*

That seemed like great advice. She took the pills that were magically laid out beside the glass and forced herself to relax. If she lay very still it didn't hurt.

Some time during the night Raoul had come into her bedroom and left the pills. He'd checked on her.

Maybe it was creepy.

Maybe it was…safe.

She let the thought drift and found it comforting. No, it was more than that, she thought. He *cared.*

For Claire, the concept of care was almost foreign. She'd been an unwanted baby. Her mother had done her best by her, but there'd been little affection—her mother had been too stressed taking care of the basics. Claire had been a latchkey kid from the time she could first remember, getting home to an empty house, getting herself dinner, going to bed telling herself stories to keep the dark at bay.

She'd gone to bed last night aching and sore and battered, but so had Raoul. She'd seen the bruises. She was under no illusion that he was hurting almost as much as she was, and he must be far more traumatised.

And yet he'd taken the time to check on her during the night. He'd thought about her waking in pain and he'd done something about it.

'I'm a sad woman,' she said out loud. 'One act of kindness and I turn to mush. And he owes me. I saved his life. Or I think I did.'

'You did.'

The voice outside the door made her jump.

'Can I come in?'

'I...yes.'

She tugged the bedcovers up to her chin and Rocky assumed the defensive position—right behind the hump of her thigh, so he could look like a watch dog but had Claire between him and any enemy.

And he could be an enemy, she conceded as he pushed open the door. He was back in his army gear. It was a bit battered and torn but it was still decent. He was wearing khaki camouflage pants and a shirt. His shirt was unbuttoned at the neck, his sleeves were rolled back to make him a soldier at ease, but he still looked every inch a soldier. He

was shaved and clean and neat, but he still looked…
dangerous.

He was carrying juice.

'You have great refrigerators,' he told her, and
the image of a lean and dangerous soldier receded
to be replaced by…just Raoul. The guy with the
smile. 'I poured myself some juice and then thought
I might check if you were awake. It seems presump-
tuous to forage in the fridge without my hostess's
consent.'

'Forage away,' she said. 'You gave me drugs.'

'They're *your* drugs.'

'They're Marigold's drugs,' she told him. 'But
I'm taking them anyway.' She struggled to sit up,
and found with one arm it was tricky. But then she
had help. The juice was set on the bedside table as
Raoul stooped and put an arm around her, pushing
a pillow underneath.

He was so close. He smelled clean. He felt…

Yeah, don't go there.

'How sore? Scale of one to ten?' he asked, withdrawing a little.

And she hated him withdrawing, even though it
was really dumb to want him to stay. To want him
to keep holding her.

How sore? Less since he'd walked into the room,
she thought. How could a woman focus on her arm
when *he* was there?

'Maybe five,' she managed. 'Compared to about
nine last night. Five's manageable.'

'It'll ease. The pills will take off the edge.'

'How do you know?' she asked curiously, and he shrugged.

'I'm in the army. Accidents happen.'

'And sometimes…not accidents?'

'Mostly accidents,' he told her, and gave that lop-sided smile that was half-mocking, half-fun.

She liked that smile, she decided. She liked it a lot.

'I've been in the army for fifteen years and never had to put a single sticking plaster on a bullet hole. But broken legs and dislocated shoulders, cuts and bruises, stubbed toes and hangovers…as first-aid officer for my unit I've coped with them all. Actually, make that especially hangovers.'

'Why did you join the army?' She was propped up now. She'd taken her pills. Maybe she should settle down and sleep again until the pills worked, but Raoul was here, and she hadn't seen anyone for four months—surely that was a good enough reason for wanting him to stay? It surely wasn't anything to do with how good he looked in his uniform. And how that smile twisted something she hadn't known could be twisted.

'Lots of reasons,' he told her. 'The army's been good for me.'

'Good *to* you or good *for* you?'

'Both. Has this island been good for *you*?'

'I guess.' She thought about it for a moment and then shook her head. 'Maybe not. Six months is a long time. You just heard me talking to myself. I do that a lot. I guess I'm starting to go stir-crazy.'

'The least your employers could do is give you a decent bedroom,' he told her, looking round at her bare little room in disgust. 'You have bedrooms here that are so opulent they could house a family of six and not be squashed, and you're in something out of *Jane Eyre*.'

'Hey, I have my own bathroom. I bet Jane never had that.' She smiled, the pain in her arm receding with every second—and it had nothing to do with the drugs, she thought. It had everything to do with the way this man was smiling at her. 'But every now and then I do sneak into one of the guest bedrooms,' she conceded. 'They all have fantastic views. Rocky and I read romance novels and pretend we're who we're not all over again. But I'm here to get my life back to normal, not indulge in fantasy.'

'You can't stay here,' he told her.

She took a couple of sips of juice and thought about it. 'I have a contract.'

'The contract doesn't hold water. It's unsafe to leave you here alone for six months and now the radio's smashed.'

'I can get a new one.'

'Which could get smashed, too. When we figure out a way to evacuate me, you need to come, too.'

'I can't just walk out.'

'I assume you can contact Don and Marigold?'

'I...yes. When I get satellite connection again.'

'Or when you get to the mainland and email or phone them. You've been injured. You have no reliable means of communication. Any lawyer in the land will tell you you're within your rights to terminate your contract. And,' he said, and grinned, 'I happen to know a lawyer right here, right now. Don't be a doormat, Claire Tremaine.'

'I'm not a doormat.'

'I know that,' he told her.

And here came that smile again. *Oh, that smile...*

'I had proof of that yesterday,' he continued. 'But for today you're allowed to be as doormat-like as you want. And speaking of wants...would you like breakfast in bed?'

'No!'

'Just asking,' he said, and grinned and put up his hands as in self-defence. 'Don't throw the porridge at me.'

'Porridge?'

'I found oats,' he told her. 'And maple syrup. It's a marriage made in heaven. It's on the stove now.'

'I thought you said you weren't going to forage without my permission.'

'I didn't need to forage for these guys. Like the eggs last night, they jumped right out at me. Want to share?'

'I...' She stared at that smile, at those crinkly eyes, at that magnetic twinkle, and there was only one answer. 'Yes, please,' she told him. And then she added: 'But not in bed.'

Because breakfast in bed with this guy around… Some things seemed too dangerous to be considered.

The transmitter was indeed useless.

They stood in the ruins of the radio shack and stared at the shambles and Raoul said, 'What on earth was he thinking? He could have had half of this set up in the safety of the house.'

'But it would have been only half of this set-up.'

Claire was dressed and breakfasted. The painkillers were working; indeed they might not be needed as much as she'd feared, for with her arm held safe in the sling the throbbing had eased to almost nothing. She'd walked outside with him to see the damage. The wind had ceased. The shack holding the radio transmitter was a splintered mess, debris covered the terracing, but the storm was over.

'He wanted to take over one of the rooms in the house,' she told Raoul. 'But Marigold wouldn't have it—a nasty, messy radio transmitter in her beautiful house. So he planned to build proper housing, but of course he wanted it straight away, so he was forced to use this.' She looked ruefully at the mess. 'This was an old whaler's cottage, but it's been a long time since any whaler came near the place.'

'Or anyone else?'

'The supply boat comes once a week. They didn't come this Monday because of the storm. I expect they'll come next week, unless the weather's bad. That's why we have decent supplies.'

'Fishing boats?' he said, without much hope, and she shook her head.

'I've never seen any. I see an occasional small plane, out sightseeing.' She hesitated. 'You're thinking of rescue. Are you sure your friends won't realise you were on a boat and be searching?'

'I'm sure,' he said grimly. 'There were reasons I wanted to be alone. I seem to have succeeded better than I imagined.'

'Hey,' she said, and she touched his shoulder lightly, a feather touch. 'Not completely,' she said. 'You're stuck with Rocky and me. Want to come to the beach?'

'Why?'

'To see if anything's been washed in from your boat.'

'You need to rest.'

'I've had four months of resting,' she retorted. 'Come on, soldier—or can't those bootees make it?'

He was wearing Don's sheepskin bootees. He stared down at his feet and then stared at Claire.

She smiled her most encouraging smile and turned towards the cliff path. Maybe she should be resting, she thought, but there was a reason she was pushing him to come with her.

While Raoul had been in charge—while there'd been things to do—Raoul's smile had been constant. He'd buoyed her mood. He'd given her courage. But now, standing in the ruins of the only way to get messages to and from the island, his smile had disappeared. She'd heard bleakness and self-blame in his voice.

He'd helped her, so the least she could do was help him back. Maybe she should dislocate the other shoulder. She grinned, and he caught up with her and glanced across and saw the grin.

'What? What do you have to laugh about?'

'You,' she said. 'I might need to put a training re-gime in place if you're not to get miserable. You're stuck here for at least five days…'

'I can't stay for five days.'

'Five days until the supply boat's due,' she said inexorably. 'But Marigold has a whole library of romance novels, and Don has fishing magazines, so cheer up. Meanwhile, let's go see if anything's left of your boat.'

Rosebud was an ex-boat.

The last time he'd seen Tom's boat she'd been upturned in the surf. Now she was nothing more than a pile of splintered debris on the storm-washed beach.

The radio shack and *Rosebud* had held his only links to the mainland and both were smashed. He looked out at the still churning sea and knew he had a lot to be thankful for—but at what cost?

'Will your friend be very upset?' Claire asked in a small voice.

He thought of Tom, and thought of the new boat he could buy him, and he thought Tom would give him heaps of flak and enjoy buying a new boat very much.

'I guess,' he said.

'Is it insured?'

He hadn't even thought of insurance. 'Probably. I don't know.'

'Will you have to cover the cost? Oh, Raoul…'

And she slipped her hand into his with such easy sympathy that it was impossible for him to say, *No, it's okay, the cost of this yacht is hardly a drop in the ocean of my fortune.*

Why would he say that when she was holding his hand and looking up at him with concern?

Um…because otherwise it was dishonest?

Maybe it was, he thought, but she held his hand and he liked it, and he thought if he was to be stuck here for days then he wouldn't mind being treated as an equal.

Time enough to be treated as a royal when he got home.

And the thought struck again. His grandparents… They'd have heard by now. They'd be grief-stricken, appalled and terrified.

Something must have shown on his face, because the hold on his hand tightened.

'It's okay, Raoul,' she said softly. 'You can't help any of this.'

'I could have.'

'Yeah, but that's in the past. You can't do a thing about that now. Focus on the future.'

'Like you have? Should I go find me a rock to sit on for six months?'

'You can have this one if you like,' she told him. 'I'm over it. Hey, is that a boot?'

It was. Rocky had found it. He was standing over it, wagging every bit of him in excitement. Raoul let go Claire's hand—reluctantly—and went to see.'

One boot. It was half hidden under a clump of seaweed.

'Let's see if we can find more,' Claire told him, and they hunted at the high tide mark and found the other, washed in after he'd kicked it off in the water. It was dumb, but their find made him feel a whole lot better.

Could a guy with boots walk home? Maybe not, but when they were cleaned and dried he wouldn't be dependent on Don's slippers. And when he was finally taken off this rock…

'You'll look very nice for the journalists,' Claire told him, and he looked at her sharply.

'Journalists?'

'You think if someone finds you that you'll slip back into Hobart unnoticed? Storm…wrecked yacht…marooned in the middle of Bass Strait…' She brightened. 'Hey, maybe you could sell it to the tabloids. All it needs is a sex angle and you could maybe make enough to pay for your friend's yacht.'

A sex angle…

The comment had been flippant. Off the cuff. It had been all about tabloid newspapers and what sold. It wasn't anything to do with what was happening to them.

So why did it seem to stand out? Why did the words seem to echo?'

What *was* it about this woman that was making his senses tune in to nuances that shouldn't be there? She was injured, vulnerable, alone. He had no business thinking of her in any way other than as someone who'd saved his life and was stuck on this barren, rocky outcrop with him until help arrived.

Think of something else—fast.

He bent and picked up a battered piece of timber, the painted registration number of *Rosebud*, and tried to think of a way he could get a message to the mainland. A way he could get a message to his grandparents.

He tried not to think of the woman beside him, of how she made him feel.

'Chuck a message in a bottle?' she asked.

He looked sharply up at her. She'd better not be able to read his mind, he thought. His thoughts were too tangled, and somewhere in there was the vision of Claire as he'd first seen her, struggling in the water towards him, holding him, her lovely chestnut curls tangled wetly around her face.

Claire...

Yeah, empty the mind fast, he told himself. What had she said? A message in a bottle?

'I suspect your supply boat might be faster,' he said, and she grimaced.

'You're right. Your grandparents will be very frightened?'

'They'll know I won't have gone AWOL.' *As will half the world.* He thought of the rumours that would be circulating. His country had had recent threats centred on the throne. The current thinking was that they had come from a crazy fringe organisation with no resources. Marétal was a small player on the world stage, but his disappearance followed by silence would have the media in a frenzy. His grandparents would be beside themselves.

No boat for almost a week…

'If we had the internet we could try and make a crystal radio set,' Claire said thoughtfully. 'I had a friend who made one once.'

'Good idea,' he told her. 'Except we *don't* have the internet and crystal sets receive but don't send. But if we had the internet we could email.'

'Oh.'

'But good thinking.'

'Don't patronise me,' she muttered.

He grinned. She really was extraordinary. 'I guess we could always burn the place down,' he said, deciding to join her in the planning department. 'If the fire was big enough and we did it during the day the smoke would be seen for miles.'

'Yeah, and if it wasn't noticed…?'

'Is there a cave in any of these cliffs?'

'I don't know about you, soldier,' she told him. 'But Rocky and I don't take kindly to caves. We like our comfy beds. And how would I explain a fire to Marigold? I'm caretaker for this place. Burning it down doesn't exactly come into my job description.'

'It was just a suggestion,' he said hastily.

'A bad one.'

'Okay, a bad one.'

'Hmmph.'

They stared at the sea some more. She was so close, Raoul thought. She was obviously thinking.

He should be doing some thinking. He *was* thinking. It was just that the woman beside him was taking up a whole lot of his thinking room.

'What about an SOS in the middle of the island?' she said, and he hauled his thoughts back to sense when his thoughts really didn't want to go.

'SOS…?'

'We could do it in rocks,' she said. 'There's a flat plateau behind the house. It's strewn with small rocks. We could organise them into an SOS. I'm thinking by tomorrow sightseeing flights might start again from Hobart. A plane might fly across.'

'Do they always fly across?'

'There aren't many,' she told him. 'It's winter. Tourists who pay money for flights will be thin on the ground and we don't have a weather forecast so it might be a lot of effort for nothing.'

He thought about it. SOS. The universal cry for help. Was it justified?

They were both well. They had enough supplies to keep them fed for as long as they were stranded and the house was more than comfortable.

'It'd be for your grandparents' sake,' Claire said, watching him. 'And you might get charged for the cost of the rescue.'

He might.

The cost would be negligible compared to the costs his country would be facing trying to locate the heir to the throne.

Claire was watching him thoughtfully. 'Is it just for your grandparents?' she asked, and he thought about telling her.

I'm royal and there'll be a worldwide search...

Not yet. For some unknown reason a voice in the back of his head was pleading, *Not yet.* She thought he was an equal. A soldier, nothing more.

She'd been battered by people who'd treated her as trash. She was feisty and brave but she'd retreated to this island, hurt.

He didn't want her retreating from *him*. He knew he'd have to tell her, but now the voice was almost yelling.

Not yet. Not yet.

'There'll be a fuss and a half when I get off this island,' he told her. 'Part of me thinks I should just stay. But the fuss has to be faced some time, and my grandparents...they'll be pushing for a search, no matter what the cost.'

And that was the truth, he thought. When he

thought of the resources they'd be throwing at it...
At *him*... And his two bodyguards... They'd be
being vilified and it wasn't their fault. Short of burning down the house, he had to try everything.

'Let's do it,' he said shortly, without answering
her question, and she looked at him curiously.

'There's stuff you're not telling me.'

'I'm ashamed of myself.'

'Would the army rescue you?'

'Yes.' That would be the best outcome, he
thought. If the army could slip in and take him off
the island...

'An SOS seen by sightseers is going to hit the
media,' she told him. 'Are you prepared to have
your picture taken?'

'I guess it'll be both of us.'

'Not me,' she told him. 'Not in a million years.
I'm hiding, remember? If you get taken off by a
crew of SAS forces abseiling down with parachutes
and stun guns I'll be hiding in Don's basement. Tell
them you were taken in by a hermit with a beard
down to his ankles who fires at the sight of a cam-
era. Better still...' She hesitated. 'Better still, just
wait for the supply boat.'

'I don't think I can.'

'Really?'

'Really.'

She looked at him long and hard. Then she sighed
and picked up his waterlogged boots.

'Okay, then,' she told him. 'Let's go dry some boots and organise some rocks.'

He organised rocks. Claire sat on a rocky ledge at the edge of the plateau and watched.

It was kind of peaceful. The wind had died completely. The weak winter sun was warm on her face. Today was one of the few days she'd had here when the weather made her think this was a wonderful place to stay.

Or maybe it was the company. Maybe it was because the ache in her arm was fading. Maybe it was because she and Rocky were safe and yesterday had made her realise how wonderful 'safe' was.

Maybe it was because she was watching Raoul work.

He worked…like a soldier. He'd decided a small SOS wouldn't cut it—he needed to work big. So first off he'd cleared an area the size of a tennis court. That alone had been huge. Now, the rocks he was heaving weren't small. One-handed, Claire couldn't have begun to help, but even if she'd been two-handed it would have been a big ask.

Raoul had simply set to work, heaving rock after rock. After the first half hour he'd stripped to his waist. He sweated a bit as he worked. His body glistened in the sunlight.

A girl could waste a lot of hours watching that body, Claire thought, and as there was little she could do to help she might as well enjoy it.

She did enjoy it.

She'd spent four solitary months here. She'd only seen the guys on the supply boat—two guys in their sixties, salt-encrusted to their toenails, bearded, weathered, cracking up at their own jokes as they tossed her supplies onto the beach and left her to cart them up to the house.

They hardly talked to her—they were men in a hurry, trying to get their run done and get back to Hobart and the pub. They couldn't know how important they'd become to her—two harried boatmen and fifteen minutes' terse conversation, mostly about the weather.

And now she had her very own guy here, to look at all she wanted, and who could blame her if she was enjoying it very much indeed?

'You're making it very big,' she ventured, and he tossed a few more rocks and wiped the sweat from his forehead with the back of his hand. He was magnificently tanned, she thought, or maybe he was permanently bronzed.

He was gorgeous.

'Last S,' he said, and headed to a pile of rocks that loomed over the plateau. He climbed the rocks as if he'd been bred on cliffs, sure and steady on the shale. This was the high point of the island. He gazed down at his efforts and gave her the thumbs-up.

'Want to see?'

'I don't think I can.' She couldn't get the full effects of his artwork from ground level, but climbing the loose rocks with one arm would be asking for trouble.

'That's what I'm here for.' He slid down the slope, reached her and held out his hand. 'Your servant, ma'am.'

'I'm very sure you're not,' she said a bit breathlessly, and he smiled.

'You saved my life. You've taken me in and fed me. Believe me, Claire, I'm your servant for life.'

And he drew her upright and she was too close. But then he turned and started up the shale again.

A part of her didn't want to be tugged up the shale. It wanted to stop exactly where it was and be held.

But that wasn't Sensible Claire thinking. It was Dumb Claire. And hadn't she made a vow to be Sensible Claire forever?

Tomorrow, she told herself. Or the next day. Whenever the SOS worked. Then she'd be alone again and she could be as sensible as she wanted.

But Raoul was tugging her up the rocks, holding her tight, making sure she didn't slip, and the feeling of him holding her was making Sensible Claire disappear entirely.

Sense would have to be left to the soldier.

'What do you think?'

They'd reached the top. He turned and held her at the waist—in case she slipped?—and she forced herself to stop focusing on the feel of his hands and look down at his handiwork.

He'd cleared the plateau. The rocks he'd used were seriously big. No one could fly over and miss the message he'd made.

He could be rescued today, she thought. A plane could fly over right now and within an hour a rescue chopper could arrive from the mainland. He'd be gone.

She shivered.

'You're cold,' he said, and curved his arm around her as if he could keep her warm just by holding her.

As indeed he could, she thought ruefully. Even hot.

'I've been doing manual work. You should have stayed inside.'

'But I love hard work,' she managed. 'I can sit and watch people do it for hours.'

Wrong, she thought. *I can sit and watch you...*

'Inside now, though,' he told her. 'You need to rest.'

'You're the one who was battered for two days.'

'So I was. So we both need to rest. And then... Do you have any movies on that very impressive entertainment system?'

'Indeed we do.' She thought for a bit, which was kind of hard, because he was holding her and he was really close and his chest was bare and his skin felt...

Um…what was she trying to think of? Movies. Movies would be excellent.

'Actually, they're mostly on the net,' she told him. 'And we have no net with the communications down. But we do have a few oldies but goodies on DVD.'

'I'm all for oldies but goodies. Popcorn?'

'Possibly not. Potato chips and nuts?'

'My favourite. You want me to help you down from this rock or would you like me to carry you?'

And what was a girl to say to that?

Luckily Sensible Claire hadn't completely disappeared. Luckily Sensible Claire said that this guy had had a physical battering and carrying a load—*her*—down the loose rocks would run every risk of disaster.

'I'll walk,' she said, and Dumb Claire almost cried.

CHAPTER SIX

THEY BOTH HAD a sleep. Then Raoul foraged in Don's cellar while Claire cooked a simple pasta dish.

He showed her what wine he'd chosen and she pretty near had kittens. 'Do you know how much that's worth?'

'No.' Then he looked at the dusty label and grinned. 'Though I can guess.'

'Raoul, it'll be half a week's salary.'

'But I could be dead. And Don owes you. He's stranded an employee with no back-up on a deserted island. Hey, and you're a lawyer. We're safe.'

'Right,' she said dryly, but she stopped arguing. Who could argue with that smile?

They curled upon the sofa and ate dinner, and Claire found chocolate, and the wine was truly excellent.

There were three settees in front of the vast TV screen, but two were elegant and only one was squishy and right in front, so it seemed foolish not to share.

They watched *African Queen* and then *Casablanca*. The wine was still amazing. The fire crackled in the hearth. Rocky snoozed by the fireside. They hadn't bothered with lights as the day faded to night. The television and the fire gave enough light.

And then the movie ended and they were left with the glowing embers of the fire.

'Another one?' Raoul asked as Humphrey Bogart walked away in the fog.

Claire was too busy sniffing to answer.

'I guess not,' Raoul said thoughtfully, and produced a handkerchief and dried her cheeks.

And she had enough sense left—*just*—to recognise the linen.

'That's one of Don's monogrammed handkerchiefs.'

'There goes another week's salary,' he said, and smiled into her eyes. 'I can't think of a worthier cause.'

'Raoul…' She should pull back, but he didn't. He traced the track of her last tear and suddenly things intensified. Or maybe they'd been intensifying all day and now they were too aware of each other, too warm and safe, too…*aware*?

Wrong word. There must be another, but Claire couldn't think of one. Actually, she couldn't think of anything but Raoul and how close he was.

She put her own hand up and touched his face— the bronzed skin, the creases at the corners of his eyes, the raw strength she saw there. And something inside her wanted. Badly wanted.

'Raoul,' she whispered again, and her body seemed to move of its own accord. Closer.

'Claire…'

'Raoul…'

Raoul's smile had faded but his hands were still tracing her cheeks. When he spoke his voice sounded ragged. 'I'm aware, my amazing Claire, that you're alone on this island apart from Rocky, and that Rocky doesn't seem to be standing guard right now. Don deserves to be tossed in jail for leaving you defenceless, and I will not take advantage. But…' He hesitated. 'I *would* like to kiss you. So, in the cold light of day…'

'It's night.'

'In the warm glow of night,' he continued, and put his finger under her chin and raised her face to his. 'Would you like to be kissed?'

'You ask me that after *Casablanca*?'

'I know I don't rate beside Humphrey.'

'*How* do you know?'

'Just guessing.'

And she managed a smile back. Sort of. 'I'd have to see.'

'Have you ever kissed Humphrey?'

'No, but I've watched him kiss. He's pretty good. It's no small order to try and match him.'

'You're asking me to try?'

'No,' she said, and her voice was pretty much a whisper. She was feeling melty. Warm. Safe. Loved?

It was a dumb feeling—a mockery, a lie. How could she feel so deeply so soon? But it was there just the same, and there was no way she could ignore it.

'No,' she said again. 'I'm not asking. I'm ordering.'

And then there was nothing to be said. Nothing at all. Because he was taking her into his arms—gently, because of her injured arm. Or maybe gently because there was no way this man would force himself where he wasn't wanted. She knew him hardly at all, but she knew that about him at least.

And she knew more. She knew how he'd taste. She knew how he'd feel. She knew how her body would respond as their lips met, as the heat passed from one to another, as her whole body seemed to melt into his.

She didn't know how she knew, but she did. It was as if her whole life had been building to this moment. It was as if he was the other half of her whole, and finally—finally—they'd come together.

It was a dumb thought. Theirs was a fleeting encounter, she thought, with what little of her mind she had left to think. This man was a stranger.

Except right now he wasn't. For this moment, on this island, he was everything she needed and more.

And caution was nowhere.

He kissed...but what a kiss.

He hadn't expected to be blown away.

He'd expected a kiss he'd enjoy. He'd expected—or hoped for—warmth, arousal, passion.

He hadn't expected his world to shift.

It did.

Was it shock?

Was it the fear of the last few days?

Was it that Claire had rescued him?

Who could say? But somehow being with this woman had changed something inside him, and whatever it was it felt huge.

He'd been in the army for years. He'd worked with feisty women—women with intelligence and honour and courage. Back home in Marétal he'd met some of the most beautiful women in the world. Society darlings. Aristocracy and royalty.

Beauty and intelligence weren't mutually exclusive. He'd dated many of those women and most he still called friends.

Not one of them made him feel like Claire was making him feel now.

He'd known her for less than two days. This was just a kiss.

So how did it feel as if breaking apart from her would break something inside him?

And, amazingly, she seemed to feel the same. Her body was moulding to his and her hands cupped his face, deepening the kiss. She was warm and strong and wonderful, and the feel of her mouth under his was making his body desire as he'd never felt desire.

This wasn't just a kiss. It could never be just a kiss. This was the sealing of a promise that was unvoiced but seemed to have been made the moment she'd crashed into him out in the water.

Claire.

If she wanted to pull back now he'd let her. Of course he would. He must, because this was a woman to be honoured.

Honour.

With that thought came another, and it was a jolt of reality that left him reeling.

This woman had saved his life. She'd been injured, battered, drugged, all to save his sorry hide, and now she was sharing her place of refuge with him.

Right now he wanted her more than anything he'd ever wanted in his life, but...

But. The word was like a hammer blow in his brain.

But he was a man of honour...

A prince...

He hadn't even told her who he was. If this went further she'd wake up tomorrow and know she'd been bedded by the heir to the throne of Marétal.

There'd be consequences, and consequences had been drilled into him since birth.

Bedding a woman he'd just met...

But how could he think of consequences? He was kissing Claire and she was kissing him back. How could he think past it?

How could he draw away?

* * *

She wasn't sure how long the kiss lasted. How did she measure such a thing? How could she think of trying to measure? All she knew was that she was kissing and being kissed and she never wanted it to end.

His arms were around her, tugging her body to him. Her breasts were crushed against his chest.

It felt so right. It felt as if she'd found her home.

Raoul. Her head was singing it—an ode to joy. *Raoul.*

Was it just that she'd been stuck alone on an island for four months? Was this some sort of Robinson Crusoe syndrome?

Their passion was pretty much overwhelming her. She seemed to have too many clothes on. Raoul definitely had too many clothes on.

Almost involuntarily her hands moved to the front of his shirt, tugging…

And his hands caught hers and held them.

He put her away from him and it nearly killed him. Every nerve-ending was warring with the caution that had been instilled in him since birth.

But he wasn't only fighting that caution. There was also a voice hammering inside, pounding out the fact that this was uncharted territory. This woman was special.

This woman had the means to slice through the carefully constructed armour he'd developed ever since his parents died. He didn't need anyone. He'd learned that early. And yet when Claire had surged through the surf to save his life... Yes, he had needed her, and somehow with every moment his body was telling him he needed her more.

But honour demanded that he step away. Honour and the need to rebuild that armour.

And was there a touch of fear in there as well?

No!

She wanted to scream it.

Don't stop. Please don't stop. I want to get close. So close...

But he was putting her back from him. She could see passion in his eyes, a desire that matched hers, but she could also see an almost desperate control.

'Claire... We can't.'

'Why not?'

'It's too soon.' His voice was almost a groan. 'Hell, I want to—I'd be inhuman not to—but you've been injured. You're still shocked and so am I. You're on this island by yourself. I won't take advantage.'

'What are you talking about? You wouldn't be taking advantage. We're both adults.'

'If we'd known each other for such a short time on the mainland...' He had her shoulders, was searching her eyes. 'Claire, would you be sleeping with me tonight or would you be saying wait a little?'

'I don't believe this.'

'I don't believe I'm saying it either. Claire, more than anything in the world I want to take you to my bed right now. But I won't. It's not just honour. It's sense. In the army—'

'What's this got to do with the army?'

'Everything,' he told her. 'And nothing. But in the aftermath of battle there's often emotional meltdown. What we've been through is the equivalent. We can't take this further until you're sure.'

And his words made her stop.

I'm sure.

She wanted to scream it from one end of the island to the other, but all of a sudden she wasn't.

He was being sensible. She hated him for it, but he was right.

If the weather blew up again they could be marooned together for weeks. Sense said that she had to keep her emotions under control.

She didn't want to be sensible.

She drew back, feeling foolish, emotional and, yes, if she was honest, humiliated. And he saw it. He reached out and touched her face again, but this time his touch was different. It was a feather touch. It was a caress all on its own.

'Don't feel like that,' he told her. 'Claire, I'm trained to recognise my emotions. I'm trained for sense.'

'And I'm not?'

'I don't know,' he told her. 'All I know is that the

way I'm feeling about you is scaring the heck out of me.'

'So you'll run?'

'Only as far as another movie.'

'Raoul…'

'Claire.' He touched her lips. 'You are truly beautiful. You are truly wanted. But we both know that sense should have us building six-foot walls.'

'I guess…' she whispered, and he smiled at her, that smile that undid every single thing he said about sense.

'I *know*,' he said, and it nearly killed her that he was right.

Somehow she slept that night. Somehow she made it to breakfast. Somehow she swallowed her humiliation and got on with getting on.

But she didn't know whether she wanted a plane to come or not.

At dawn she was already tuned in to the sound of engines, but it was midwinter and the storm would still be fresh in people's minds. That storm had swung up from the Antarctic seemingly with no warning. Tourists would therefore be delaying or cancelling their sightseeing flights, so a plane was unlikely.

Somehow she had to figure a way to get through this without going nuts. She needed a way of facing Raoul and not wanting him…

After breakfast—a meal full of things unsaid,

of loaded silences—she decided to cook. Cooking had been a comfort to her forever, so why not now?

'Muffins,' she told Raoul.

'Muffins?' He'd been distant over breakfast. He was obviously finding the going as hard as she was. It seemed up to her to find a way through it.

'If you want fresh food on this island you need to cook,' she told him. 'And I even have frozen herbs. So if we want muffins for lunch…'

There was a silence, and then, 'Do you have apples?'

'Tinned.'

'Hmm.' He considered. 'That might be a challenge, but I'm up for it. You make your muffins. I'll make *tarte tatin*.'

'*Tarte tatin?* With tinned apples?'

'I'm a camp cook extraordinaire.'

'Wow!' She stared at him. He was back in Don's pants and the T-shirt that stretched too tight. They'd showered before breakfast. His hair was still damp. He was still a bit…rumpled.

The man could cook.

So they cooked, but if she'd thought it would make things easier between them she had been dead wrong.

She watched as he made pastry from scratch, his long, strong fingers rubbing butter into flour as if he'd been doing it all his life.

Wanting him was killing her.

'Who taught you to cook?' she managed. 'Your

grandmother? If your mother died when you were so young…'

'Many people taught me to cook,' he told her. 'I was never neglected.'

'It sounds like you came from a wonderful community.'

'I did,' he said, but his answer was curt. Maybe it hurt to go there. 'And you?'

'I taught myself to cook.'

'Not your mother?'

'Mum was on her own. I was an accident when she was eighteen and she had a hard time keeping me. She struggled with depression but she did her best. Early on I learned I could make her smile by having something yummy ready when she got home. She used to clean at the local hair salon and she brought home magazines that had got too tatty. I learned to cook from those magazines. It took me ages to accept that some ingredients were too expensive. I'd write a list, and get fed up when she'd come home with cheddar cheese rather than camembert—but she tried.'

'You both sound…courageous.'

'We weren't courageous. We just survived. Until…'

'Until?'

She shrugged. 'Until Mum couldn't survive any more. When I was fifteen she lost the fight.' She dredged up a smile. 'But by then I could cook— and cook well. I could look out for myself, and I was pretty intent on a career where I could afford good cheese.'

'So you became a lawyer?'

'As you say. I pushed myself hard and libraries were my friend. Study was my friend.'

'Hence the French?' She'd spoken French in the water. He'd hardly remembered, but he remembered now.

'What else was there to do when the nights were lonely?' she asked. 'Italian. French. Chinese. And cooking—which seemed the most important of the lot.'

'You speak Italian, French and Chinese?'

'Doesn't everyone?' She cocked her head to one side. 'Soldier?'

He couldn't resist. *'Was ist Deutch?'* he demanded. *What about German?*

'Ich spreche Deutsch. Aber ich kann nur verstehen wenn langsam gesprochen wird.'

I speak German but I can only understand if people speak slowly.

'Sie sind eine erstaunliche Frau,' he said.

You are an amazing woman.

She grinned. 'Well, I can understand that. You're not bad yourself. German, French, English... Any more?'

'There might be,' he admitted. 'I have smatterings of a lot. Marétal's official language is French, but it's pretty multilingual, plus years in the army means I've travelled. Want to go head to head with how many languages we can swear in?'

She chuckled. 'No way. Rocky would be shocked. Besides, if we're competing I'd rather cook. Your *tarte tatin* against my muffins?'

'Who gets to judge?'

'Rocky, of course,' she told him. 'And he's a very satisfactory judge. If it's edible he'll give it ten out of ten every time.'

The wind was getting up again. Whitecaps topped the ocean. It was becoming more and more unlikely that there'd be any joy flights over the island today, so therefore why not relax and have a cook-off?

It was an unlikely pastime. If anyone had told him three days ago that he'd be marooned on a rocky outcrop, cooking *tarte tatin* beside a woman he was trying not to go to bed with, he'd have thought they had rocks in their head.

But that was what was happening.

He cooked, but a good half of his attention was on the woman beside him. She was struggling a little, sparing her bad arm. He'd told her she should rest, that she could watch *him* cook, and she'd reacted as if he'd said she had two heads.

'And let you lord it over me when your *tarte* comes out of the oven? In your dreams, soldier. This is battle!'

It was hardly a grim battlefield. They were watching what each other was doing. Learning. Pausing to watch the tricky bits. And finally they were re-laxing.

They were talking about the island and her four months here. The things she'd seen. Her personal quest to rid the island of every bit of fishing line that had ever been washed up there—'*Do you know what damage tangled line can do to wildlife?*' The books she'd read. The story of Rocky—how she'd chosen him from the rescue shelter the day before she'd left for the island and how she'd spent the first month trying to persuade him to come out from under her bed.

She talked of her childhood. She talked of her admiration for the legal assistance organisation she'd worked for and how she never should have left. She talked of its scope and its power. She talked of the disaster of her time in Sydney.

She tried to get him to talk to her.

'Is it the army that's making you silent?' she asked at last. 'They say returned soldiers are often too traumatised to speak. Is that you?'

'That's a blunt question.'

'Hey, I had a mother with depression. I learned early not to sugarcoat things. "Mum, how bad are you feeling? Scale of one to ten." That's what I learned to ask. So there you go, Raoul. How traumatised are you—scale of one to ten?'

'I don't think I'm traumatised.' Though that wasn't exactly true. There had been engagements that he didn't want to think about, and she must have seen it in his face.

'You don't want to go there?' she asked, and he shook his head.

'No.'

'And when your boat turned upside down…?'

'I was too busy surviving to be traumatised. And then along came a mermaid.'

'How very fortuitous,' she said primly. She'd finished her muffins—they were baking nicely—and she'd started on a lasagne for dinner. She was feeding pasta dough into a machine, watching with satisfaction as the sheets stretched thinner. 'So what about your childhood?'

'I don't think I'm traumatised.'

'Not even by your parents' death.'

'I was very young. I can hardly remember them, and my grandparents took over.'

'But you don't want to talk about it?'

'No.'

'Fair enough,' she said, and went back to her lasagne.

He thought she wouldn't press. She didn't sound in the least resentful that she'd just told him all about her and he wasn't returning the compliment.

He *should* tell her about himself.

It would change things, though. Of course it would. The decision not to go to bed with her had been the right one, he thought. Claire could be… his friend?

So if she was just his friend why not throw his background out there and see how it altered things?

He could say... *The reason I wasn't traumatised by my parents' death is that I hardly saw them. They were socialite royals. They had a good time while their child stayed home with the servants. Even after they died my grandparents were distant. The reason I cook is that I spent much of my childhood in the kitchens. The head cook called me 'mon petit chou' and hugged me as I licked cake mixture from a spoon. The kitchen was my security.*

But he didn't say it. To admit to being royalty was huge, and what was between them seemed strange, tenuous, uncharted territory. Their friendship had happened so suddenly he didn't know how to take it. He only knew that this woman seemed like a miracle. She'd appeared in the water when he was about to drown. She'd given him life. But then, on land, she'd turned out to be...different. As different a woman as he'd ever met.

A woman who made him feel...vulnerable?

A woman he wanted to protect.

So he said nothing. He fell back into silence as they cooked and Claire was silent, too. She was restful, he thought. She was a woman he could come home to.

Or not leave?

A woman he could stay with for the rest of his life.

Whoa. Where had *that* come from? How crazy a thought was that?

Far too crazy. He needed to get away from here and rebuild his armour—fast. He was a loner—wasn't he?

'Done,' she said, popping her lasagne into the oven and closing the door with a satisfactory click. 'That's timed for dinner.'

'Time for a rest?'

'Why would I want a rest?'

'Your shoulder,' he said tentatively. 'Doesn't it hurt?'

'Only when it jerks, and I'm not jerking. And I don't feel like a rest.'

'Then how about a walk?' More than anything else he wanted to take this woman into his arms and carry her to bed, but there was still a part of him that was rigidly holding back. If a plane arrived now and he was airlifted off the island—what then? What next?

He had to go home.

He could take her home with him.

The thought came again from left field, mind-blowing in its craziness. What was he *thinking*? He'd known this woman for *how* long? *Take it easy,* his sensible self was ordering, and he had to listen, even if it almost killed him.

'A walk would be good.'

She was eyeing him speculatively and he wondered if she'd guessed what he was thinking. Probably she had, he thought. She seemed…almost fey.

No. In some weird way she seemed almost an extension of himself. She'd know what he was thinking.

And maybe she agreed. If she was indeed some deep-linked connection to himself then she'd be as wary as he was. And as off-balance. And she'd understand his need to rebuild his armour.

'We could go and see the seals,' she suggested, and he tried to haul his thoughts back into order and believe a walk to the seals would be good. It was a poor second to what he'd prefer, but it had advantages.

They were full of muffins. *Tarte tatin* and lasagne were waiting in the wings for dinner. The wind had died a little and Rocky was looking hopeful. A man had to be practical instead of emotional.

But it nearly killed him to nod and agree.

'Excellent idea. Let's go see some seals.'

The seals were on the far side of the island. By the time they reached them Raoul was counting his blessings that he'd found his boots and they were clean and dry enough to be useful.

Claire, on the other hand, was wearing light trainers and was leaping from rock to rock like a mountain goat. Okay, not quite like a mountain goat, he conceded as he watched her. With her arm firmly in its sling, as long as they were off the slippery gravel she was as lithe and agile as a fawn.

'You've been practising,' he told her, and she looked back at him and grinned.

The wind was making her curls fly around her face. She looked young and free and...happy. Something had lifted, he thought, remembering her face two days ago. Yes, she'd been in pain, but there'd been other things going on behind the façade. Things he didn't know yet.

Things he might never know?

How had his presence lifted them?

'I've had four months to practise,' she told him. 'Rock-hopping has become my principal skill.'

'Do you regret coming here?' If he was honest he was struggling to keep up with her. It wasn't strength that was needed here, it was agility—and she had it in spades.

'Yes,' she said honestly. 'I was battered and my pride was in tatters and I wanted to escape. But next time I want to escape, please tell me to choose a tropical island with cabana boys and drinks with little umbrellas.'

'The weather's got you down?'

'The isolation. Rocky's an appalling conversationalist.'

'So will you leave now?'

'How can I leave?' She surveyed a large rock ahead of her, checked it out for footholds and took a jump that had him catching his breath. But she was up on top without even using her hands. Maybe the mountain goat analogy was appropriate after all.

'Because it's not safe,' he told her. 'You're not safe here.'

'I'm safer than walking through King's Cross at three in the morning. That's the red light district of Sydney.'

'So there's another place you oughtn't to be.'

'My chances of getting mugged here are practically zero.'

'And your chances of slipping on a rock and faling and being stuck out here alone, with no one to find you…'

'And being eaten by the seagulls,' she finished for him. 'I thought of that. I'm very careful.'

He watched her tackle another rock. 'Define "careful".'

'I'm safe.'

'You're not safe.'

'You think I should stay in the house and read and cook for the entire time?'

'Don shouldn't have left you out here alone. You shouldn't have come.'

'Okay, I shouldn't have come,' she told him. 'It was a whim when I was feeling black, and, yes, Don told me there was another guy here. I talked to him via radio before I came. He seemed decent. He didn't tell me he intended leaving.'

'And now you're alone with no radio.'

'I can get it fixed. I have the authority.'

'It's smashed. It'll take weeks. Claire, you need to come off the island with me.'

There was silence at that. She paused on the top of the rock she'd reached, looked at him for a long moment and then shook her head.

'Not with you. I'll think about it. But I guess I agree about leaving. Without a radio it's not safe, but the supply boat can take me off. I can stay in Hobart until it's fixed.'

'It's still not safe.'

She turned and started climbing again. 'Define "safe". I thought I was safe in a nice lawyerly job in Sydney and I almost ended up in jail. How safe's *that*? And how safe are *you*? Where's your next assignment? War zones in the Middle East? Do you want to pull out of *them* because they're not "safe"?'

'I'm no longer in the army.'

She stopped then, and turned and stared at him. 'No?'

'No.'

'So the uniform…?'

'Probably needs to be returned—though it does have a few rips. My last pay might be docked.'

'I thought you were AWOL.'

'I'm not. I'm on indefinite leave until I can be discharged. That's why I was out in the boat. I had a last talk to my commanding officer and then went down to the harbour to think things through.'

'So they might not even be worried about you?'

'They'll be worried.'

She nodded, surveying his face. There was a long silence.

'You're not happy about leaving the army?' she said and he shrugged.

'No.'

'But you're safe?'

'Yes.'

'You don't want to be safe?'

'It's time I went home.'

'Because…?'

'My grandfather's in his eighties and he's getting frail. My grandmother worries. They need help.' How simplistic a way was *that* of saying what was facing him?

'Oh, Raoul…'

The wind caught her hair, making her curls toss across her face. She brushed them away with impatience, as if the way it impeded her view of him was important. She was watching his face. She was asking questions she wasn't voicing.

'It's tearing you in two to leave the army,' she said softly, and there was nothing to say to that but the truth.

'Yes.'

'What will you do?' she asked at last, and he shook his head.

'I'm not sure yet. There will be things…that have to be done.'

'Things you don't want to think about?'

'Maybe.'

'Like me when I leave this island.'

'The army's been good to me,' he said. 'This island hasn't been all that good to *you*.'

'Hey, it's taught me rock-climbing skills. It can't be all bad.' She smiled at him—a gentle smile that somehow had all the understanding in the world in it. 'Maybe we're alike,' she said. 'Maybe we just need to figure where our place is in the world and settle. Stop fighting to be something we're not.'

'Like you…'

'A corporate lawyer? Rising above my station? I don't think so. As I said, I'm thinking of getting my job back doing legal assistance, working for the socially disadvantaged. I fit there.'

'That sounds bitter.'

'It's not meant to be.' She took a deep breath and turned to face out to sea. 'I know I'm not socially disadvantaged any more,' she said. 'But I also know where I don't fit. I tried to take a big step from my background and failed. I know where my boundaries are.'

'So if someone asked you to take a huge step…?' Why had he asked that? But he had. It was somehow out there—hanging.

'Like what?' She looked at him curiously. 'Like Don offering me this job? That was pretty crazy.'

'I don't know. Something adventurous. Something fun. All jobs don't have crevices waiting for you to fall into.'

'No,' she said thoughtfully. 'They don't. But it

behoves a woman to look for crevices. It behoves a woman to be careful.'

And she turned and leaped lightly to the next rock.

He stood watching her for a moment, thinking of crevices.

Thinking of the royal family of Marétal.

Thinking that Claire Tremaine would think—like him—that royal life might well be one huge crevice.

CHAPTER SEVEN

THE SEALS WERE AMAZING—once you got over the smell. Claire had been there often enough not to be blown away by the aroma, but she watched Raoul's reaction and grinned.

It was a rocky inlet, far too dangerous to swim in or beach a boat, but the seals loved it. The rocks were covered by a mass of seals, mostly pups, basking in the weak afternoon sunlight or bobbing in the sea. A couple of massive bull seals were sitting at either end of the cove, watching over the nursery with brooding power.

'Those guys fight a lot,' she told Raoul. 'They think they're great, but when they're busy fighting I've seen younger males pop in and take advantage. Power doesn't always outweigh brains.'

'You've noticed that?' He shook his head and went back to screwing up his nose at the stink. 'You'd have thought these guys would have sorted a sewerage system.'

'Maybe they don't have a sense of smell. Trust an ex-soldier to go all sensitive on me. Next time we'll pack some air freshener. But come and see.'

This was her favourite place on the island. Her favourite thing to do. The young seals were being joyous, tumbling in and out of the water, practising their diving, sleek and beautiful under the translucent sea and bouncing and boisterous on the rocks. The best vantage place was further round—a rocky outcrop where she could see straight down into the depths. She wanted to take Raoul's hand and tug him to where she intended to stand, but she managed to hold herself back.

She had no right to tug him anywhere, she thought. He was being sensible and she must be, too.

She thought suddenly of the young bull seals, charging in when their elders were fighting, taking their fill of the females and then leaving. That was what men did, she reminded herself.

But not Raoul. Raoul was different?

Or not different. Just…kind? Not leading her anywhere he didn't intend to follow?

So she didn't take his hand. She headed up to the outcrop herself and willed him to follow. As, of course, he did.

Despite his sense, he was a young bull at heart, she told herself, but she couldn't quite believe it. He was so like her. He was a soldier, a kid with no parents, a man with courage and with strength.

Maybe she could turn and touch his face…

'What's happening?' Raoul asked sharply, and she hauled her attention from thinking about Raoul to the surface of the water.

All the seals were suddenly gone. The water, filled moments ago with tumbling pups, was suddenly clear.

And as they stared a crimson smear bloomed up to the surface. A silver-grey mass swirled underneath and then was gone.

Even the seals out on the rocks stilled. The world seemed to hold its breath.

'Shark,' Raoul said, and his hand slid into hers. *Shark.*

She watched the crimson stain spread on the water. She thought of the seal pup, its life over almost before it had begun.

She thought of Raoul in the water two days ago and shuddered.

'You don't swim while you're alone here?' Raoul asked, almost casually, and she shook her head.

'No.'

'I mean…not on this whole island?'

'Only…only when I'm pulling dumb sailors out of trouble.'

'Have you seen this happen before?' His tone was still casual.

'I…yes.' Of course she had. Seal breeding areas were a natural feeding ground for sharks.

'The island's not very big. So there are sharks… *everywhere*?'

'Obviously not where *you* fell in,' she retorted, trying to make her tone light.

'But you knew…?'

'No biggie. My lasagne will be cooked. You want to go back and have dinner?'

'Half my kingdom,' he said, and now he'd forgotten to be casual. His voice was thick with passion. 'It's yours. My life... You swam into these waters to give me that.'

'Seeing as you've already spent more than half your kingdom, drinking Don's wine and smashing your friend's boat, that's not much of an offer.'

'Whatever it is, I mean it. Claire...'

'No biggie,' she said again. 'Leave it, Raoul. I might even have done the same for Felicity.

'You're kidding?'

'Well, I might have swum slower,' she admitted. 'I might not have minded if her toes had been a bit nibbled. But, yeah, I'm pretty certain I would have had to do it for Felicity. Not that I'd have enjoyed it.'

'Like you enjoyed rescuing me?'

She gave him a long, assessing look and she grinned. 'I did,' she admitted. 'There are aspects of rescuing you that I enjoyed very much indeed. But I'm putting them on the back burner. You've decreed we be sensible, and sensible we shall be. Home to lasagne, soldier, and then bed. Alone.'

They ate lasagne and Raoul's truly excellent *tarte tatin*. They watched *National Velvet* and *The Sting*. They were excellent movies. They had trouble paying them the attention they deserved, but they had staying power.

At some time during one of the movies they edged together on the settee. There was only one blanket, and the snacks had to be within reach of both of them. It was only sensible to stay close.

The movies came to an end and they followed them with a nature documentary. Birds in Africa. Raoul thought he should abandon the television and head to his separate bed, but he didn't want to break the moment, and it seemed neither did Claire.

So they both pretended the birds were riveting. She was leaning against his shoulder, nestled against him. His chin was on her curls. She fitted into the curve of his arm.

She felt...*right*.

And he had to tell her.

Somehow he'd found himself with someone who must surely be the most wonderful woman in the world. Though that was a crazy thought, he decided. There must be other wonderful women.

But he'd met many women. His grandmother had pushed many at him, many had launched themselves at him, and he'd even pursued some himself.

None came near this woman. None made him feel like this.

But he'd been acting on a lie. Oh, he'd *told* no lies, but this relationship was moving fast, moving hard, moving to places he'd never been before and it was based on trust.

Claire thought he was a soldier. Claire thought he was a kid with no parents.

That much was true.

Claire thought his background wasn't so different from hers, and he'd let her think that.

He sat with Claire nestled against him and let things drift. He was savouring the feel of her, the silence, the peace of this place. He knew what was waiting for him in the outside world. The palace would be frantic. There'd be a worldwide hunt. The media would go nuts when he reappeared.

He'd like to hurl the SOS stones from the plateau and stay here forever, holding this woman in his arms. But his responsibilities were unavoidable. He'd walked from the barracks and climbed on board *Rosebud* because he'd felt overwhelmed by the responsibilities facing him, and those responsibilities hadn't disappeared.

His country needed him.

And Claire?

She had him confused. The armour he'd so carefully constructed didn't seem to be working against her.

He was a loner. He had to walk away from her—a plane might arrive tomorrow—but when he left he didn't want her to think these few days had been a lie.

She needed honesty.

He touched her cheek and she stirred and smiled—a smile that was so intimate it almost tore his heart.

He knew he made her smile. She made *him* smile.

'Claire…?'

'Mmm…'

All he wanted was to take her into his arms, make love to her and block out the outside world. Put it off. Take every moment of this time and let Claire find out when finally she must.

But *must* was now if she was ever to trust him.

'Claire,' he said softly, and traced her cheek with his forefinger. 'Let me tell you who I really am.'

Royal.

The word was drumming a savage beat all through her body.

Royal.

She should have known.

How *could* she have known? She couldn't possibly. It wasn't as if he'd come out of the surf wearing a crown or something.

She choked on a sound that might have been laughter but wasn't. Raoul's hold on her tightened, but he didn't say anything. After telling her he was simply holding her, waiting for her to take it in.

And Raoul holding her was part of the dream, too.

This whole thing had been a dream.

Hauling a soldier out of the water, the deadly peril, the lifesaving stuff, being carried up to the house, her shoulder being righted, the care, the comfort and then the kiss. The beginnings of love? That was what it had felt like, she acknowledged, but of course it had been an illusion. A two-day fantasy that had culminated in the greatest fantasy of all.

A prince!

She felt very close to hysterics and her thoughts were all over the place. It was frogs who were supposed to turn into princes. Not gorgeous half-drowned soldiers who were perfect just the way they were.

'I never should have kissed you,' she managed, because she had to say something. Somehow she had to move forward from this moment.

'Because…?'

'Because then you'd still be a frog. And I liked my frog.' She took a deep breath and pushed herself up. She sat and looked at him in the firelight. He gazed calmly back—her soldier, the man she'd felt seeping into her heart, the man she'd thought was within her orbit.

'If we're talking fairytales…'

'*Cinderella*'s another one,' she said. 'And I never understood that story. She got to change rags for tiaras, but everyone would always know there were rags underneath.'

'You're not in rags. And tiaras aren't compulsory.'

And suddenly the conversation had changed. It was all about them. It was all about a future neither had even dared to consider until this moment. A nebulous, embryonic future which suddenly seemed terrifying.

'I shouldn't believe you,' she said at last. 'Why *do* I believe you?'

'Because in telling you I risk losing you,' he said.

He wasn't moving. He was leaning back on Marigold's sumptuous cushions, watching her, giving her the space she didn't want but desperately needed.

'And the last thing in the world I want to do is lose you.'

'You never had me.'

'No,' he told her. 'But, Claire...I'm starting to think that what we have might be...possible...'

And she snorted. How did she feel? Humiliated, she thought. And lost. As if she'd lost something she'd never had.

'After two days?' she managed. 'I don't think so.'

'It's true. If I hadn't told you then you'd be still lying in my arms, and that's all I want. But I had to tell you some time. Claire, does it have to make a difference?'

'A difference to what?' Although she knew.

'A difference to me seeing you again, off the island. A difference to taking this friendship further.'

'You're kidding me, right? A kid from Kunamungle? A baby with no known father? A kid brought up on the wrong side of the tracks—and even though Kunamungle's small, believe me, there *is* a wrong side of the tracks? A woman who couldn't even get accepted in a legal firm? A lawyer with no background, no money, no aspirations, and now with the stigma of fraud hanging over her head? You're telling me you're heir to the throne of Marétal and asking if it makes a difference to a possible friendship? *Yes*, Your Highness...'

'Don't call me that.'

'Yes, Your Highness, it *does* make a difference.'

'Why?' he said evenly. 'Claire, nothing has changed. I still feel—'

'It doesn't matter how you feel,' she snapped. 'Haven't I always known that? It doesn't matter how you feel or what you want or what you hope for. It's what you *are* that matters.'

The night was too long. The house was too big. Their bedrooms were too far apart and Raoul knew he had to leave her be. Claire had retired to a place he couldn't reach, and after breakfast the next morning—another silent breakfast—she headed off for a long walk with Rocky.

'If a plane comes I'll come back,' she told him. 'Otherwise I could be some time.'

'Like Oates of the Antarctic, heading out into the snow for the last time?'

'Hardly,' she snapped. 'I'm not about to die in the snow because of one prince.'

And she stomped off towards the cliffs.

He was left thinking that he really wanted to go with her. But he had deceived her. The least he could do was give her space. This would probably be their last day together. Surely a plane would come soon.

Followed by a chopper to take him off the island. Followed by the rest of his life.

It was his last day with Claire and she'd left.

He couldn't blame her. Swapping roles, he might have walked himself, he thought. And then he really thought about it. If he'd been a soldier and only a soldier, and she'd been heiress to a throne, how would he have reacted?

He wouldn't have walked. He'd have run.

Even if it had been Claire?

Maybe.

He didn't do ties, and royalty would have terrified him too.

Maybe Claire was right, he conceded. *Cinderella* was a sexist fantasy. Put a woman in a beautiful gown, give her a tiara and a palace and expect her to live happily ever after? It wouldn't work for him—although the gown and tiara analogy had to change—so why would it work for Claire?

It wouldn't.

So that was the end of that.

But at the back of his mind was a harsh, unbendable wish. The end? It couldn't be. It mustn't be because he wanted her.

So soon?

And there was another problem. With the threat of a plane arriving at any minute emotions seemed to have become condensed. He was so unsure where this was going. He felt as if his armour had been cracked, and it scared him, but the more he saw of Claire, the more he was prepared to risk.

Too much was happening, too fast. The responsibilities he faced back in Marétal were enormous. The adjustment he was facing made him feel ill. He didn't need emotions messing with what was ahead of him.

He didn't need Claire.

So if a plane arrived today he might well never see her again. A prince from Marétal and an Australian lawyer? How many chances would they have to meet?

Never.

He thought suddenly of his grandmother's demand that he bring a woman to the Royal Anniversary Ball.

Claire?

Polite society would have her for breakfast, he thought. His grandmother alone would be appalled.

Impossible. The whole situation was crazy.

The house was empty, echoing. He found himself straining for the sound of a far-off engine, a plane, the signal of the end of something that had barely started.

Surely it didn't have to end yet.

He abandoned the house and headed down to the cove where Claire had swum to save him. The water was calm today, but the beach was littered with debris from the storm and from the battered *Rosebud*. The yacht was now little more than matchsticks. He searched the beach, looking for anything he could salvage for Tom, but he was doing it more to distract himself rather than because Tom would want anything. Tom was free, off climbing his mountains.

Two weeks ago Raoul had said goodbye and had been consumed with regret. He'd wanted that kind of freedom.

He couldn't have it. And now he couldn't have even a friendship with Claire.

Unless he didn't treat her as Cinderella.

His thoughts were flying tangentially, and all the while he was distracted by the thought that a plane could arrive at any minute. Finally he climbed along the side of the cove, where the waves from the open sea crashed against the cliffs and he couldn't see the sky from the south. If he couldn't see the plane it didn't exist, he told himself, and he almost smiled. It was a game he'd played when he was a child, when he'd been forced to sit through interminable royal events. He'd worked out how to look interested and still disappear inside his head, dreaming of where he'd rather be.

He had no choice as to where he'd be.

Did he have a choice in who he'd be with?

Claire...

She was a beautiful woman and she made him feel as he'd never felt before. Yes, it was too soon to think about the future, but his head wasn't giving him any leeway. He wanted her.

She was an intelligent, courageous woman who

was street-smart. She was a woman who spoke Italian and French, and he had no doubt she was fluent. The phrase he'd flung at her in the water had been gasped, yet she'd understood it without hesitation.

Marétal's official language was French, but natives spoke a mix of Italian and French with some of their own words.

Claire was smart. She'd pick it up.

She didn't want to be Cinderella. Who would?

And he... What did *he* want?

Besides Claire.

He forced himself to think sideways, to think of the life he wanted as a royal.

He wanted to make a difference.

Claire would never want a job that involved tiara-wearing and nothing else. Well, neither did he. If he had to go home—and he did—then he needed to make something of it.

With Claire?

Don't think down that route, he told himself. *Don't even think about hoping.*

But the ball... He had no doubt his grandmother would still insist it go ahead. He also knew that if he didn't organise a partner his grandmother would attempt to do it for him, and the thought was suddenly so claustrophobic it almost choked him.

Claire was still front and centre. He thought of her as she could be. Someone not royal from birth but truly royal as she deserved to be. Why *shouldn't* the woman who'd saved his life be his partner at the ball? Even if nothing came of it, it would be a night of fantasy. A night he'd never forget.

She'd never agree. Why would she?

She needed a job to do. She needed to be needed.

Something colourful caught his eye, caught on a pile of seaweed. He stooped and picked it up.

It was a tiny plastic building brick figure. It was a miniature construction worker, complete with a hard hat and a spanner in his hand.

He'd noticed it on the shelf above Tom's bunk, taped fast to stop it falling. He'd commented on it on their first day's sailing and Tom had grinned, a bit embarrassed.

'That's Herbert. I've had Herbert since I was six years old. He's my good luck talisman. Where I go, he goes.'

He'd noticed him when he'd gone aboard again five days ago and thought of Tom, gone to climb mountains without Herbert.

He had Tom's good luck talisman.

And imperceptibly, ridiculously, his spirits lifted. 'Sorry, Tom,' he told his absent friend. 'Take care on those mountains, because Herbert's about to work for *me*.'

Maybe…

He dusted the sand from Herbert and tucked him carefully into his pocket.

'Come on, then, Herbert,' he told him. 'I'll send

you on to Tom when you've done your job here. But now *I* have need of you. Let's see what happens if we offer a lady a job.'

'A job.'

Claire had walked her legs off. She'd been tired, her arm had ached, and finally she'd turned back. She'd known she had to face him some time. She might as well get it over with.

She'd found Raoul in the kitchen, flipping corn hotcakes. He had smiled at her as if nothing had changed. He'd asked politely about her walk and then watched in satisfaction as she'd eaten his hotcakes. Okay, she was discombobulated, but a woman could be discombobulated *and* hungry.

And then he'd said he wanted to offer her a job.

She stared at him, all six feet of gorgeous Prince, and felt herself cringe. What was he saying?

'I don't think royal mistress has ever been one of my career choices,' she said carefully.

'Who said anything about you being a royal mistress?'

'I kissed you. I know it's dumb, but now it makes me feel smutty.'

'You could never be smutty.'

He reached over the table to touch her face but she flinched.

'Don't.'

'Touching's out of order?'

'Until I get my head around this, yes.

'Claire, you're my friend. You're the woman who saved my life. You're also the woman who attracts me in a way I don't understand yet.'

'You lied.'

'I didn't lie,' he said evenly. 'But neither did I tell you the truth. Why would I? It would have made a difference. If we'd lain exhausted on the sand after you helped me out of the water and I'd said, *By the way, I'm a prince,* wouldn't it have changed…everything?'

'Yes.' She might as well be honest.

'Well, maybe that was what my dumb attempt to sail in dangerous weather conditions was all about. For the last fifteen years I've been in the army. Working in a tight-knit unit with men and women focused on a common mission. I've been one of many. But the moment I return to Marétal— the moment I step out of army uniform—things will change. As they would have changed if I'd told you.'

'I thought you were like *me.*'

'How could I be like you? You're beautiful.'

She flushed. 'Don't, Raoul.' She closed her eyes and he could see her trying to tear her thoughts away from the personal. 'The SOS…' she said. 'Your grandparents…'

'They're the ruling monarchs. The King and Queen.'

'So the heir to the throne is missing, presumed drowned?'

'Probably presumed kidnapped,' he said grimly.

'There have been threats. We haven't taken them too seriously—my country seems too small to attract terrorist interest—but now I'm missing they'll be being taken very seriously indeed. I can't imagine the resources being thrown into searching for me.'

'But they won't think of here.'

'They won't think I'm dumb enough to take out a boat without letting anyone know, and Tom doesn't know his boat is missing. I'll have a lot of humble pie to eat when I get home.'

'So you're hoping a plane will come today?'

'Yes,' he said gently, and made an involuntary move of his hand towards hers. And then he pulled back again. 'I have to hope that—if just to stop the anguish of my grandparents and the money being spent on searching for me. But when I'm rescued… Claire, I'm asking if you'll come with me.'

'To this job?'

'Yes. Can I tell you about it?'

'Oh, for heaven's sake…' She got up and filled the kettle, then took a long time to organise cups for coffee. 'I must have been banged on the head. This isn't real.'

'It *is* real. Claire, I can't leave you here. This place is unsafe. You have no radio transmission, and as far as I can see it could take weeks to get technicians here to fix the system.'

'I can order a smaller unit…'

'Which will come by the next supply boat—which might or might not arrive depending on the weather. And you'll still be alone. If you slipped on the rocks… If you swam…'

'I won't swim. Are you crazy? The water's just above freezing.'

'You're quibbling. It's not safe for you to be here and you know it. Don should know it. If you don't tell him then I will.'

'Okay.' She turned to face him, tucking her hands behind her back like an errant child facing a stern teacher. 'I shouldn't have come here,' she conceded. 'Like you, I made a spur-of-the-moment decision and I accept it's not safe. So, yes, I'll lock up and go to Hobart—but that's as far as I'm going. You head back to your royal fantasy. And I'll…'

'You'll what? Look for a job? I'm offering you one.'

'Raoul…'

'I won't let this go,' he said, steadily and surely. 'Claire, this thing between us…I've never felt anything like it and I can't walk away. But I've scared you silly. Plus, it's too soon. We've been thrown together in extraordinary circumstances. If you were Sleeping Beauty I'd see you for the first time, fall in love with you on the spot and carry you away to my castle for happy-ever-after. But that story's always worried me. After the initial rush of passion, what if she turns out to have a fetish for watching infomercial television? Or women's wrestling? What if she insists on a life devoted to macramé?'

'I don't know what macramé is,' she said faintly.

'Exactly. And therein lies the brilliance of my plan.'

'The job?'

'The job,' he agreed. 'Claire, I have a problem. I've upset my grandparents enormously. In three weeks there's a ball to celebrate their fifty years on the throne. I imagine that right now it's been cancelled, but as soon as I turn up alive my grandmother will resurrect it. She's indomitable.'

He paused. Claire handed him a mug of coffee. He took a sip and grimaced, as they both did when they tasted this coffee. There was nothing like caterers' blend to make you rethink your caffeine addiction. But even the truly awful coffee wasn't enough to distract him from what seemed such a nebulous plan.

'And…?' she prodded.

She really shouldn't talk to him of the future, she thought. He was a royal prince. He had nothing to do with her.

Except she'd kissed him and she'd wanted him. Her body still did want him, regardless of what her mind was telling her. Was desire an excuse for keeping on talking?

'I'm expected to have a partner for the ball,' he said in a goaded voice, and she decided she needed to stop wanting straight away.

'So you're going to ask me?' she managed. 'Cinderella.'

'I told you—I don't buy into Cinderella.'

'And I don't buy into balls. Or royalty. Or—on a basic level—being surrounded by people who think they've been born better than me.'

'I would *never* think that.'

'You don't need to. It's bred into your genes. You look down your aristocratic nose...'

'That's insulting,' he said, suddenly exasperated. 'Can you get off your high horse and listen to a perfectly good job offer?'

She thought about it, or tried to think about it, and then decided the only way to think about anything was not to look at Raoul. *Prince* Raoul, she reminded herself savagely, and she plonked her cup hard on the table, spilling about a quarter of the contents, and stared into what remained.

'Shoot.'

'Shoot?'

'Go ahead. Tell me about your job so I can refuse and get on with my life.'

'Claire...'

'Talk,' she ordered. 'I'm listening, but not for very long.'

CHAPTER EIGHT

BUT IN THE end she did listen.

In the end it sounded almost reasonable.

'A couple of years ago one of the Australian soldiers I was on an exercise with told me about his son,' he told her. 'The boy was faced with a lengthy jail term for being immature, gullible and in the wrong place at the wrong time. It seems the legal assistance service you worked for helped him escape conviction and gave him another chance. To my shame I'd forgotten it until you mentioned it, but I know we don't have such a service at home—legal help for those who can't afford lawyers. Claire, if I'm to return as more than a figurehead I'd like to institute a few reforms—reforms long overdue. I've never had the authority to make those changes, but maybe it's time for a line in the sand.'

'A line…?'

'You'd be the beginning of my line,' he told her.

She dared a glance at him and discovered he was smiling. She went back to her coffee fast. 'What do you mean?'

'I mean you would accompany me back to Marétal. You'd be greeted by my grandparents as the woman who saved the life of the heir to the throne. And I'll say I've offered you a job—investigating the need for such a service in our country.'

He held up his hand to prevent her instinctive protest.

'Claire, hear me out. My idea is that you'd spend a month talking to our public services, talking to the people high up in the judicial system, assessing whether our system is similar enough to the Australian system for something like legal assistance to work. Given you'll have access via me to whoever you want to speak to, a month should be sufficient to give you an overview. And then you'd go home.'

She did raise her eyes then. She stared up at him in astonishment. 'I'd go home?' she managed.

'Once you've spoken to my people I'd ask—through diplomatic channels—that you have the same access to yours. Then I'd ask that you put forward a proposal for Marétal. It might be six months' work to put together such a proposal, but that six months…' He hesitated. 'Claire, we could use it. We could just…see.'

'See what?' She was having trouble speaking.

'See where we are at the end of six months,' he told her. 'See if we feel the same as we do now. See whether this relationship has legs.'

'Legs…' she muttered, and managed a sort of smile. 'Slang in how many languages?'

'How many do *you* know?' He shrugged. 'Claire, you're smart, you're strong, you have solid legal training and you know enough about the needs of low-income earners to be empathic. You're what our country needs.'

'Others could do the job.'

'I want you.'

And there it was, out in the open, staring at them like a two-headed monster.

I want you.

She could say the same.

She couldn't.

'The ball…' she muttered, and he gave a slightly shame-faced grin.

'That's the pay-off,' he told her. 'A favour, if you like. Claire, I can't pretend there's nothing between us. There is. We both know it. If you come back to Marétal I won't deny there's an attraction.'

'You think I'd move into your palace? Not in a pink fit.'

He grinned. 'How did I know you'd say that? But my plan's more practical. We could find you a nice little apartment in the legal quarter of the city. You'd start work. There'll be a flare of publicity when we arrive, but it'll settle. It'll be suspected that we have a relationship, so there will be media interest, but it won't be over the top.' His grin turned a bit lop-sided. 'I *have* had girlfriends before.'

She tried not to smile back. She tried really hard. She failed.

'Really?'

'Really.' And then he did reach out and take her

hand, and she knew she should pull back, but she couldn't. Not when it was Raoul.

'And thus we come to the brilliance of my plan,' he told her, and she blinked.

'Brilliance?'

'I could escort you to the ball. My grandmother couldn't object because you're the woman who saved my life. She'll stop throwing society darlings at me for a while. She and my grandfather will have a wonderful ball, which they'll thoroughly enjoy, without my grandmother watching me every minute of the night to see who I'm dancing with. You'll get to wear a very beautiful dress—did I tell you I owe you at least a gown? And then you could go home.'

She stared at him blankly. 'Home. To Australia. I don't get it.'

'You should,' he said gently, and his hold on her hand tightened. 'Claire, I think I'm falling for you,' he said. 'But after this short time of course I can't be sure. To be honest, relationships have always scared me. I've been a loner all my life and I'm not sure I can stop being a loner. If you're feeling the least bit like I am you'll be feeling just as uncertain. Plus, the thought of royalty scares you. I'm not surprised—it still scares *me*. But this scheme gives us time. By the night of the ball you'll have had weeks in the country. Then there'll be the ball, which will be royalty at its most splendid. Afterwards you'll get on a plane and you'll spend a few paid months back in Australia investigating the intricacies of legal assistance on Marétal's behalf. And thinking about me—us.'

'Thinking about you…us?'

'That's my hope,' he said, and threw her one of those gorgeous grins that made her heart twist.

Oh, my... Where were her thoughts? They were all over the place. *Think,* she told herself. *Stop sounding like a parrot and get real.*

'The whole idea's crazy,' she managed.

'Tell me why.'

'If you want to find out about our legal assistance scheme you should send one of your own people out here to see how it's done.'

'I could,' he agreed. 'But if I gave the job to any of my senior people they'd come with prejudices. They'd think they'd be doing the old school lawyers out of jobs, and the younger staff wouldn't have the clout to ask the right questions. Claire, you wouldn't be changing anything. All you'd be doing at the end of six months would be handing over a concept that our people could work with.'

Our people. How had he suddenly transformed into a royal? she thought. Last night he'd been a soldier and her friend. Okay, being honest, he'd also—almost—been her embryo lover. Being honest with *herself,* if he'd taken her to bed she would have gone and gone willingly.

But today…

'If I gave the job to any of my senior people…'

He was speaking as a prince. He *was* a prince. He was as far from her as the sun was from the earth.

He was holding her hand.

'But why? Why me?' she demanded. 'And why now? Surely this legal assistance scheme isn't a priority?'

'It's not a priority,' he agreed. 'But it is a real need, and it's my need, too. And I hope yours. Claire, it's not safe for you to stay on this island. You must see that. Soon we'll be taken off. When we do the eyes of the world will be on us. I'm sorry, but I can't stop that. In Australia I can't protect you from media hype. In my country I can—to an extent. The palace can call in favours. Yes, there'll be speculation, but we can live with that. The line is that I met you, I was impressed with your legal credentials...'

'You don't know anything about my legal credentials.'

'I do,' he told her. 'How can I doubt that they're impeccable? Not only do I trust you, I can ensure the world will, too. Two minutes after we land in Hobart there'll be a legal suppression order thumped on the appalling Felicity and her friends. If one whisper of improper conduct comes out, your ex-firm will be faced with a libel suit so massive it'll make their eyes water. Claire, what I'm proposing is sensible, but it's not sense I'm talking. It's desire. This way you come back to my country. I won't be able to spend much time with you between now and the ball, but you'll see enough of me—and I'll see enough of you—to decide if we have the courage to take this thing forward.'

'Courage…'

'It *would* take courage,' he told her.

His fingers were kneading hers gently, erotically, making her feel as if she wanted to stop talking this minute and head to the bedroom while there was still time. But of course she couldn't. Raoul was talking sense and she had to listen.

Sense? To fly to the other side of the world with a royal prince? *Her?* Claire Tremaine?

Her head was spinning. The only thing grounding her seemed to be Raoul's hold on her hand, and surely she shouldn't trust that.

'It would take courage,' he said again, as if he'd realised her mind was having trouble hearing, much less taking anything in. 'But what I'm suggesting takes the pressure off as far as I can figure how to do that. You'd stay in my country until the ball. You'd dance with me as my partner.'

He gave another of his lopsided grins and she wished he hadn't. It made her… Well, it made it a lot harder for her to take anything in.

'It would be a favour to me,' he told her. 'It would take the pressure from me. It would make my grandparents happy…'

'That you're dancing with a nobody?'

'They can hardly think you're a nobody when you saved my life.'

'Don't you believe it.'

'Claire, stop quibbling,' he said, firmly now. 'Because straight after the ball you'll have a return ticket to Australia. Ostensibly to research a legal assistance system on our behalf. No—*really* to research a legal assistance system. That will give you time to come to terms with everything you've seen and with how you feel about me. It will give us both time. You can return to Australia with a job to do and we can both take stock of how we feel. No pressure. Your call.'

No pressure.

No pressure?

Her head felt as if it was caving in.

'You don't know what you're asking,' she managed, and he took both her hands then, tugging her so she was looking straight at him. What had happened to their coffee? Obviously that was what happened when you used caterers' blend, she thought tangentially. You got distracted by...*a prince*.

'I *do* know what I'm asking,' he told her. 'And it's a shock. To you, though—not to me. Claire, I knew the moment you pulled me from the water that your life had changed. You don't save royal princes and then get marooned on deserted islands with them for days without media hype. You *will* get media hype, and I'm sorry. But there's also this thing between us—this thing which I'm not prepared to let go. With my plan...I'm trying to rewrite the *Cinderella* story. I'm trying to figure how to get through this with your dignity as top priority. This way you'll come to the palace, you'll meet my grandparents, you'll see things as they are. Then you'll come to the ball as an honoured guest. And, yes, I'll dance with you—a lot—but in real life the Prince has to dance with others, because feelings can't be hurt. And you'll dance with others, too, because men will be lining up. And at midnight...'

'Where's my glass slipper?' she said shakily, and tried to smile.

He smiled back. 'That's where the plot changes to what it should be. At the end of the ball I'll put you back into your carriage, which won't turn back into a pumpkin, your luggage will be waiting and you'll take your return ticket back to Australia. I won't come hunting for you. You're your own person, Claire. If you take this job then you have months of secure employment, doing work my country needs. And then you can work out if you have the courage to return.'

'Why...why would I return?'

'Because, fast as this is, and even though I've known you such a short time, I suspect I'll be waiting for you.'

'But no promises?' she said, fast and breathlessly, and he nodded.

'No promises from either of us,' he told her. 'Both of us know that. But this is a chance...our only chance...to wait and see. If you have the courage, my Claire.'

'I'm not your Claire.'

'No,' he agreed. 'You're *your* Claire and the decision is yours. Will you come home with me and give us a chance?'

And what was a woman to say to that?

How could she look into those eyes and say no?

She might have courage, but her knees felt as if they'd sagged under her—and she wasn't even standing.

'Claire?' he said softly, and put a finger under her chin and raised her face so her gaze met his. 'Will you come with me?'

'Yes,' she whispered, because there was no other response. 'Yes, I will.'

And then the world broke in.

At two that afternoon a small plane swooped low over the island.

After four months of isolation the pilots of such planes, like the captains of the supply boats, seemed to have become Claire's friends. They weren't really. They were people doing their job. She couldn't talk to them, and she didn't even know their names, but she usually walked outside and waved. Sometimes they flew low enough so she could see people waving back.

They'd just finished lunch, a mostly silent meal during which too much seemed to be happening in their heads for talk to be possible. Raoul had talked of practicalities and Claire had listened, but mostly her head was full of one huge question.

What had she agreed to do?

The sound of the plane was almost a relief. She glanced out of the window and hesitated. 'If I go outside and wave they'll think I'm okay,' she told him. 'They might not even see the SOS.'

'No one can miss my SOS,' Raoul told her. 'And if you *don't* go outside we'll have people thinking you might be wounded. I didn't have enough rocks to write a detailed explanation of the problem underneath. Claire, we need to be seen. Together. I assume they know you're usually alone here? They'll see us. The wreckage from *Rosebud* on the beach is self-explanatory. Let's go.'

So he led her outside, and they stood on Marigold's Italian terrace, and Claire waved and Raoul stood silently by her side.

He seemed grim.

And as she waved for the first time it struck her. What he was asking of her was huge, but what he was facing himself was even bigger. He'd been in the army for fifteen years—a rugged life, dangerous, challenging, but obviously something he felt deeply about. He was back in his army uniform now, having decided he wouldn't risk facing the world in Don's gear. But it was more than that, she thought. In his army gear he knew who he was.

She glanced at the set lines on his face and thought again of the reasons he'd walked down to his friend's boat and set out to sea.

This was an ending for him. And end of being who he wanted to be.

The start of his royal life.

'You'll be brilliant,' she said, and he looked down at her, startled.

'What…?'

'As a prince. You'll be amazing. Look at you now—you've had three days lying around here and you could have…I don't know…rested on your laurels, played the royal Prince, ordered me around like anything…'

'As if I would.'

'Exactly,' she said. 'Instead you taught me how to make *tarte tatin*, and if nothing else ever comes of this then I thank you. You've assessed this whole situation. You came over all bossy when you told me I need to leave. But more…you thought of the legal assistance thing—and, Raoul, I know that's partly for us, but it's also for your country. You're thinking of what it needs. If you start that way you'll be brilliant. I know you will.'

'Not unless…' And then he stopped. 'No. I won't blackmail you.'

'Excellent,' she said as the plane swooped low, did a one-eighty-degree turn and swooped again, right over the centre of the island where Raoul's

SOS stood out like a beacon. 'Because we both have enough pressure on us already. All we can do is face forward and get on with it.'

CHAPTER NINE

THREE WEEKS LATER, in an apartment in Marétal's secure legal precinct, she woke where she wanted to spend the rest of her life.

She woke in Raoul's arms.

'Let me not move.' She murmured the words to herself, not daring to whisper, hardly daring to breathe. 'Let me hold this fantasy as truth.'

For this *was* a fantasy. This was where Cinderella could have her fairytale, she thought. In the arms of her Prince.

No. She wasn't in the arms of her Prince. She was in the arms of the man she loved.

And almost as she thought it Raoul woke, and the arms that had held her even in sleep tightened. Her body was spooned against his. Her skin was against his. The sensation was almost unbearably erotic. The sensation was pure…fantasy.

'I can't believe it's only weeks since I first kissed you,' he murmured into her hair. 'It feels like months. Or years.'

They'd been businesslike, as planned, even though it had almost killed them. But they'd had to be. They'd travelled back to Marétal together, but as soon as their plane had landed Raoul had been absorbed back into the royal family.

Claire was being treated as an honoured guest. The story was that she'd rescued him and he'd been fortunate enough to persuade this skilled lawyer to take an outsider's look at the country's legal system.

There'd been mutterings from the legal fraternity—'Why do we need such an overview?'—but she was young and non-threatening and the royal sanction was enough to keep the peace.

There'd been more than murmurs from the media—of course there had: *Prince trapped on remote island with glamorous Australian lawyer.* But Raoul had organised her clothes to be couriered from Sydney. She'd taken pains to appear in the prim clothes she customarily wore for work.

There'd been a lavish dinner held by the royal family to thank her formally for her heroism, and Raoul had sat by her side, but she'd deliberately dressed plainly, with little make-up and her hair arranged in a severe knot. Raoul had been charmingly attentive, but he'd carefully been charmingly attentive to the woman on his other side too, and the rumours had faded.

The media would have killed to listen in on the phone calls Raoul made to her every night, the calls she held out for, but the apartment he'd organised for her was in a secure part of the legal district where privacy was paramount.

'If I so much as smile at you in the way I want to smile at you you'll be overwhelmed,' Raoul had told her, and she'd agreed.

This was the plan. She was here to do a job—wasn't she? Nothing more. And Raoul's calls... They were those of a friend.

Except she knew in her heart they were much more. She should stop them, she thought, but she couldn't bear to.

And the calls were a mere fraction of her day. For the rest of the time she could tell herself they weren't important. She'd buried herself in the work she was here to do, and somewhat to her surprise had found it incredibly interesting. There *was* a need. She could do something useful. Paths had been opened to her through Raoul, and through the interest in her background. She'd learned a lot, fast.

What she'd also learned was how constricted Raoul's life was. He could go nowhere without the eyes of the world following.

But finally, last night, Raoul's promise to keep his distance had cracked. A plain black Jeep had driven up to her apartment and paused for maybe five seconds, no longer. A soldier had stepped out and he'd been inside her apartment before the Jeep had disappeared from sight.

If anyone had been watching—which they probably hadn't, because interest had died down—they'd simply have seen a shadow, and that shadow had disappeared so fast they could never have photographed it.

The shadow had finally risked coming.

And Claire should have greeted him formally,

as a friend—no, as an employer—but it had been three long weeks, and the phone calls had become more and more the centre of her day.

And, sensible or not, she'd walked straight into his arms and stayed.

The shadow was now holding her. He was running his lovely hands over the smoothness of her belly. He was kissing the nape of her neck. He was sending the most erotic of messages to every nerve-ending in her body.

Raoul. Her fantasy lover.

Her Prince.

'How long can you stay?' she whispered to him now. She scarcely dared to breathe the question but it had to be asked. This night had been so unwise but it would have to stop. Was this all there was? One night of passion, maybe two, before she returned to Australia?

It had to be—she knew that.

Because she needed to return. She'd known that from day one, when she'd seen the sea of photographers pointing their cameras at her. Raoul was royalty and he lived in the media glare, and even if she was ever deemed suitable for him she had no wish to join him.

Except for the way he held her.

Except for the way she felt about him.

Except for now.

Last night… It had been as if two halves had

found their whole. She'd walked into his arms and she'd felt complete in a way she'd never felt before.

Raoul had warned her he was coming and she'd made dinner. Dinner had been forgotten.

Dinner had turned into all night.

Dinner had turned into perfect.

'I'm taking all day,' he murmured into her hair, holding her closer. 'Imperatives be damned. You can't believe how much I've missed you. Holding you feels like it's making something in me complete. My Claire. My heart.'

'I can't be your Claire, Raoul. It's taken you three weeks to find an opportunity to come.'

She didn't say it as a reproach. It was simply fact. She'd learned by now how much his country needed him. But he wanted to explain.

He rolled over, propping himself above her so he could look down into her eyes. 'Claire, you know why. You didn't want to come to this country as my lover. Neither of us wanted that. We had to let the media interest die. But we can't go on this way. Maybe it's time to let the world know what's between us.'

He kissed her then, lightly on the lips. Or he meant to. His kiss deepened, and when it was done he pulled back and the smile was gone from his eyes.

'I want you,' he told her. 'I've never wanted a woman as I've wanted you. I've never needed a woman. Claire, every time we talk I'm falling deeper and deeper in love with you. My days have been a nightmare, a jumble of pressing needs, but every night I've called you, and that's what holds me together. Claire, I know it's early. I know I said you're free to go—and you are. But if you could bear to stay for longer... If you could bear to be seen by my side...'

And the world stilled.

She loved him. She knew she did. Their time on the island had been the embryo of their loving. The flight back to Marétal had made it grow. The long calls every night... The sight of him in the newspapers, discussing the needs of his country, shouldering a responsibility she knew was far too heavy for one man...

But to announce their love to the world? To let the media in?

'You could face that?' She said it as a breathless whisper and he smiled then—that smile that did her head in, the smile that wanted her to agree to anything he suggested.

Anything? Such as walking out onto the balcony and shouting to the world that they were lovers?

Staying with Raoul seemed right. But the rest... It did her head in.

'Still too soon?' he asked, sounding rueful. 'Claire, I've known you for less than a month and yet I'm sure.'

'But...' she managed, and he sighed and closed his eyes, almost as if he was in pain.

'*But*,' he agreed. 'I live in a goldfish bowl. It's a privileged goldfish bowl, but that's what it is.'

'You're doing your best to improve your bowl,' she told him, striving for lightness.

Striving to keep the underlying question at bay. Or the underlying answer. The answer she knew she'd have to give.

'The news is full of reports of the discussions you've been having with your grandparents and parliament,' she told him. 'They say you're dragging Marétal into the twenty-first century. You want parliament to have more power. You want the people to have more say. And yet the Queen is arguing.'

'My grandparents have held the rule of this country for fifty years,' he told her, following her lead, maybe realising how much she needed to play for time. 'They've wanted me to share that rule. It's come to the crunch now, though—they *need* me to share rather than *want* me to. I hadn't realised quite how frail my grandfather is and how much my grandmother depends on him. So they need me. But I've told them that if I'm to inherit the throne I'll do it on my terms. Or walk away.'

'*Could* you walk away?'

He'd hugged her around so they were face to face on the pillows—the most intimate of positions. His nose was four inches from her nose. His hands still held her waist. They were talking of something as mundane as…inheriting a throne.

'If they won't agree then I might not have a

choice,' he told her. He sighed. 'She's fighting me every inch of the way. Even security for the ball… Our security service is tiny, but it should *be* there. She refuses to have officers in the ballroom. But with so many dignitaries from so many places how can we check? The ball is for my grandparents and she insists on having her way.'

'And if she keeps insisting?' She couldn't help it, a tiny flicker of hope kindled and flared. If he could abandon the throne… If he could just be what he once had been… Raoul. Soldier. Sailor.

Lover.

'I don't know,' he said bleakly. 'I'm trying to think of a path but there's no one else to take it on. I have no cousins, and the constitution states that the country reverts to being a republic if the throne has no heir.'

'Is that a problem?'

'After so many years under a monarchy parliament's weak. Anything could happen.'

'So you're stuck?'

'I think I am.'

The flicker of hope faded. Raoul smoothed her face with his beautiful hands and kissed her on the eyelids.

'Don't look so sad, *ma mie*.' He hesitated. 'Is it possible…?' He drew back a little so he could look directly into her eyes. 'Is it possible that you've already decided you can't be with me?'

How to make him see…? 'Raoul, you know I'd stay—but three weeks…and this is the first time…'

'Because of caution. With no caution I'd have had you in my bed every night.'

'And have the whole world looking down on me?'

'Is that courage speaking?' An edge of anger came into his voice. 'Are you *so* afraid of what people will think?'

'Your grandmother made it quite clear… My dog…'

He managed a smile at that. The Queen had asked Claire to be brought to her straight from the airport. Rocky had just been released from his crate. The royal couple had been on the palace steps to greet their heir's saviour.

'It was me who dropped the leash,' Raoul said ruefully. 'After twenty-four hours in a cage he did what any dog would do. She'll warm to him.'

'He's not remotely pedigree. Like me.'

'What's the reverse of a snob? Someone who's proud of her convict ancestors? That should be you. *I'm* proud of your ancestors,' he told her. 'They produced *you*.'

She managed to smile, but the knot of pain within was killing her. The thought of what he was asking was huge. To stand beside him in the glare of publicity… To pretend to be something she could never be…

'Raoul, I can't do this. I need to go home.'

His smile faded.

'I know you do,' he said softly. 'I did know, even from the start, that asking such a thing of you was grossly unfair. I think I've always known what your answer would be. In your place my answer would be the same.'

He sighed then, and kissed her once more, his lovely hands caressing her body, making every sense cry out that here was her place. But it wasn't. It never could be.

'Don't be sad.' He kissed her eyelids again, and maybe there was the beginning of tears there for him to kiss. 'Let's pretend. Grant ourselves a little more time for fantasy. The ball is on Friday. You need to come to the palace to be fitted for a ball gown. I'm being fitted for my own uniform today. So—a fantasy afternoon with swords and tassels and tiaras and lace. Can you have fun with me? My grandparents are in the country, so we'll have the place to ourselves.' He grimaced. 'Well, that's if you don't count a hundred-odd staff, but we pay them well to be discreet. And afterwards…a picnic in the palace grounds? Out of sight of prying lenses? Rocky's more than welcome. What do you say, my Claire? A day of fantasy and fun before we accept reality?'

How should she respond? She glanced across the room to where her severe black jacket hung on the back of a chair—her legal uniform, her life after this time-out.

Her time with Raoul.

'We should end it now,' she whispered, because she had to. Because how was it fair on Raoul to keep him loving her one minute longer?

'Do you want to?' he asked, and his hands caressed her body, and he touched her lips and smiled. 'Now?'

'Raoul…'

'Another week,' he told her.

'Of one-night stands?'

'I'll take what you give me, my love,' he told her. 'Because the rest of my life is a very long time.'

So there were undertones of impending sadness and inevitability, but at some time during the next few hours Claire gave herself up to the idea of enjoying this short sweet time, taking what she could and walking away with memories.

At least that was what she told herself in the sensible part of her brain. But most of her brain was taken up with simply being with Raoul. The future was some grey, barren nothing. For now there was only Raoul—only the way he held her, the way he smiled at her, the way he loved her.

At midday another Jeep arrived discreetly at her apartment and Claire and her shadow soldier—and Rocky—slipped into the back. Then the Jeep made a circuitous journey to the royal palace, and Claire and her dog and her shadow were in Raoul's world.

They drove past the grand entrance, where the King and Queen had watched down their noses as she'd stumbled through formal greetings.

The palace was a storybook fantasy—a concoction of white stone, turrets, battlements, and heraldic banners floating from spires. The palace scared her half to death. This time, though, they drove around to the back, winding through formal gardens into a place that seemed almost a secret wilderness. The driveway curved onto gravel, accentuating the sense of country, and the Jeep finally came to a halt at a far less intimidating entrance, built between stables and a massive conservatory.

A servant did come down the back steps to greet them, but he was dressed in smart-casual. He was in his sixties, white-haired and dignified, and his smile was warmly welcoming.

'We're happy to have you back, miss,' he told her, and his tone said he meant it.

'Claire, this is Henri Perceaux—my grandparents' chief advisor,' Raoul told her. 'Anything you need to know about this country, ask Henri. On top of everything else, he's my friend. He taught me how to ride a horse when I was six.'

'That's something I've always longed to do,' Claire told him, and both men stared at her as if she'd grown two heads.

'You're Australian and you don't ride?' Raoul demanded.

'Nor do I pat kangaroos as they hop down the main street of Sydney,' she retorted. She shook her head. 'Stereotypes... Just because I'm Australian...'

'Apologies,' Raoul said, and then fixed her with a look. 'But you *can* surf, right?'

'Um...yes.'

'Then you can still be an Australian. Even if we're about to fit you with a tiara.'

'You're about to fit me with a *tiara*?'

'I've a team of dressmakers organised to discuss what you'd like to wear to the royal ball,' Henri said, sounding apologetic. 'If it's satisfactory with you, miss?'

She took a deep breath. Where was a fairy godmother when she needed one? she thought. One wave of her wand and Cinderella had a dress to die for. Cinders never had to face a team of dressmakers.

'Anything you want, they will construct,' Raoul told her. 'Let your imagination go.'

'My imagination's frozen. I don't know much besides black and jeans.'

'Then let yourself have fun,' Henri interspersed. He cast a covert glance at Raoul. 'That's a lesson that needs to be learned. You can still be royal *and* have fun.'

'Says you,' Raoul retorted.

'If I may be so bold,' Henri told him, 'I've watched your grandparents for many years, and within the constraints of their royal roles they do indeed enjoy themselves.'

'They do,' Raoul said tightly. 'But they have each other. They've been lucky.'

The palace was amazing. Over the top. Splendid. When Raoul would have taken her through the palace grounds first, thinking maybe she'd find the fabulous gardens less intimidating, the little girl in Claire made her pause.

'First things first. I'm in a palace. I need to see a chandelier.'

'They're all in the reception rooms and formal living areas,' he told her, bemused. 'Oh, my grandmother has one in her bedroom—no, make that two—but that's because she likes a bit of bling.'

'Will you show me?'

'My grandmother's bling?' he demanded, startled, and she stopped dead.

'No, Raoul, not your grandmother's bling. Your grandmother scares me. But a chandelier, none the less.'

'Which one?'

'Don't be obtuse. *Any* one.'

'Why?' he asked, curious.

'Because the only chandelier I've seen is a plastic travesty my friend Sophie hangs in her bathroom.

And even though Sophie's cut me off because of my dubious legal status, one day I may meet her again and I'd love to be able to raise my brows in scorn because I've met a chandelier bigger than hers.'

'You've truly never met a chandelier?'

'I told you—I come from the other side of the tracks, Your Highness,' she retorted.

He looked down at her for a long moment, as if considering all the things he should say—he wanted to say. But finally he sighed and shrugged and managed a lop-sided smile. 'One chandelier coming up,' he told her. 'But if we're going to do this then we'll do it properly. The ballroom.'

'There won't be people?'

'It'll be empty. Cross my heart. Who goes into a ballroom unless there's a ball?'

'Someone to polish the chandelier?'

'It's the weekend. Chandelier-polishers are nine-to-five guys, Monday to Friday.'

'You know that how…?'

'It's in the "*Boys' Own Almanac of What Princes Need to Know*". Trust me.'

'Why should I trust you?'

'Because I'm a Prince of the Blood and I love you,' he told her, and before she could think of a retort he handed Rocky to Henri to take to the stables for a romp with the palace dogs—*'I'll take good care of him, miss.'* Then he took her hand and towed her through a maze of more and more breathtaking

passages until they came to a vast hall with massive double doors beyond.

'Behold, my lady,' he said, and tugged the doors
open.

If she only saw one chandelier in her life, this was
the one to see. It was breathtaking.

Raoul flicked on the lights as he pulled open the
doors and the chandelier sprang to life. Once upon
a time it must have been fitted with candles, but
the lighting was now instant, with each individual
crystal sparkling and twinkling its heart out.

And there were hundreds of crystals. Maybe
thousands. The chandelier was a massive art form,
a work of a bygone era when such things had been
made by skilled artisans funded by the very rich-
est in the land. This was a work of joy.

She'd never seen such a thing. She stood in the
cavernous, deserted ballroom and she gaped.

'It's enormous,' she managed at last.

'There are bigger,' he told her. 'If you're interested, the world's largest is in the Dolmabahçe Palace in Istanbul. It has over seven hundred lamps,
it weighs over four tons, and they have a staircase
with balusters of Baccarat crystal to match.'

She thought about that for a moment and finally
decided to confess. 'I don't know what a baluster
is.'

'You know what?' He grinned. 'Neither do I. But

that's what our guidebook says. We include the information so we sound modest.'

She looked up again at the glittering creation and shook her head. 'Modest? I don't think so. How can you come from living in the army to living in a place like this?'

'How do you know I didn't have a wee chandelier in my rucksack?' he said.

But he suddenly sounded strained and she thought it had been the wrong question. Chandelier or not, he wasn't where he wanted to be. But then he smiled, and she knew he was hauling himself back to reality. Putting regret aside.

He tugged her around to face her and his smile was a caress all by itself. 'Claire, I refuse to let you be intimidated by a chandelier. They're useful things and that's all.'

'Useful for what?'

'For dancing under. How are your dancing skills? I'm demanding to be your partner for at least one waltz.'

'Only one?' she asked, before she could stop herself.

'It depends,' he told her. 'If I dance with you more than twice the media will have me married to you and be conjecturing on how many children we'll have. I'm not objecting, but...'

'Two dances only, then,' she said hurriedly, because she had to. 'Raoul, we need to be sensible.'

There was a moment's pause. She saw his face close again, but then it was gone. Put away. He was back under control.

'As you say,' he said tightly. 'But the waltz… Claire, the eyes of the world will be on us. Do you need a fast lesson?'

'I can waltz!' She said it with some indignation, but then relented. 'Okay, I don't move in circles where the waltz is common, but my mum could dance and she taught me.'

'I'll feel different to your mum.'

'You think?'

'Try me,' he said, and held out his arms, waltz hold ready.

And she hesitated, because more and more she wanted to melt into those arms and more and more she knew she didn't fit there. But Raoul was asking her to dance under what surely must be the second biggest chandelier in the world and he was holding out his arms…

And this was Raoul.

She smiled up at him—a smile full of uncertainty and fear, a smile that said she was falling—had fallen—so deeply in love there was no going back. A smile that said she knew the pain of separation was inevitable but for now she was so in love she couldn't help herself.

She stepped forward into his arms. He took her in the classic waltz hold, lightly, but as if she was the most precious creature in the world.

They danced.

She melted.

There was no music—of course there was no music—but the beat was right there in her heart. In his heart. She knew it. She felt it.

He held her and their feet scarcely touched the ground. He moved and she moved with him, in perfect synchronisation. How they did it she would never afterwards be able to tell.

It was as if this man had been her partner for years.

For life.

They danced in the great empty ballroom, under the vast chandelier that had seen centuries of love bloom under its sparkling lights, and that was now seeing a Prince of the Blood fall deeper and deeper in love.

And when the dance drew to an end, as dances inevitably did, the lights continued to glitter and sparkle as Raoul tilted his lady's chin and kissed her.

And as he did so a youth appeared in the doorway. He wasn't a palace employee but an apprentice to the master electrician who checked the chandelier at regular intervals.

The electrician didn't work nine to five—not when there was something as major as a ball coming up. Not when every guest room had to be checked and every facet of palace life had to be seen to work splendidly for this state occasion.

He'd finished checking the chandelier lights that morning, but was missing a spool of wire. 'Check the ballroom,' he'd told his lad. 'Make it fast.'

So the lad had slipped into the room—and stopped short.

He knew the Prince—of course he did. And the girl... This woman had been on the front pages of the newspapers for a couple of days. She'd rescued the Prince. She was here for a royal reception and to do some legal something or other. The media had reported sadly that there appeared to be no romantic attachment.

And yet here they were.

The apprentice might not be the smartest kid on the block, but he knew an opportunity when he saw it. He raised his phone and with one click it was done. Photographed. Safe.

Then he went back to report sadly to his boss that the spool of wire was nowhere to be found.

The kiss ended. They were left gazing at each other in some confusion.

I could let myself stay in these arms, Claire thought. *I could just...try.*

And if it failed? If *she* failed? This wasn't some minor fling. Breaking the Prince's heart would make her seem like a villain the world over. But the alternative...to live in a gilded cage and be judged...

She shuddered, and Raoul saw the shudder and touched her face.

'No,' he said, strongly and surely. 'Today we don't

let the future mar what we have. You know what I'd like to do now?'

'What?'

'Take you to the gymnasium and let you show me your karate skills. You did say you were good.'

'I did,' she said, because why use false modesty here? Raoul might admit that his was only the second biggest chandelier, but her karate skills were okay.

'So prove it,' he told her.

She knew what he was doing. The kiss had been intense, passionate—a kiss that claimed—and she'd stepped away in fear. She was falling so hard, so fast. How to keep her sensible self working?

But Raoul must have seen the flash of fear and suddenly emotion was taking a back seat to challenge. Karate. 'I bet you can't throw me,' he told her.

'I bet you I can. Do you really have a gymnasium?'

'Yes.'

'Just for you?'

'The staff use it, too,' he told her. 'This is a large palace and we look after our employees. But I can block out any time I want it to myself. Usually I don't, but today I took the precaution...'

'Because you want me to prove myself?'

'Claire, you don't need to prove a thing,' he told her, his voice gentling. 'You've already proved you're the woman—'

'Not another word,' she interjected, suddenly breathless. 'Not one more word, Your Highness. But, okay, let's head to this gymnasium and see if I can throw you.'

She could throw him.

He lay on his back, stunned, and looked up at the diminutive woman above him with incredulity.

At her first approach he'd allowed her to throw him. He'd learned some martial arts himself—it had formed part of his army training. Then, bemused by Claire's claim to skill, he'd performed a token block—because he suspected that, yes, she really could throw, but he was large and skilled himself, and he didn't want to hurt her pride.

That thought had lasted all of twenty seconds, which was the time Claire had needed to move in, feign an amateurish movement, change swiftly to a move that was anything but amateurish and have him flat on the mat.

She grinned down at him. 'You'll have to do better than that, soldier.'

Soldier. For a moment she'd lost the Prince thing. She was having fun, smiling down at him, laughing at the ego that had had him misjudging her.

So then he got serious. He rose and circled and thought about everything his martial arts sergeant had told him.

As a soldier Raoul was trained to work with any

number of different weapons. He could work on tactics, set up a battalion for attack, retreat, advance, camouflage, exist on meagre rations, survive with bush craft...

He could do this.

He moved in to attack, thinking how best to throw her without hurting her.

The next moment he was on his back again, and he didn't have a clue how he'd got there. *Whump!* He lay, winded, on the mat, and she was smiling down at him with the same patronising smile that said this throw had been no harder than the first.

'What the...?'

'I told you I was good,' she said, with not a hint of false modesty about her. 'Believe me?'

'Teach me that throw.'

'Really?'

'Please,' he said humbly, and she put down a hand to help him up.

He gazed at it with incredulity, and then grinned and put his hand in hers. She tugged him up, and he let her pull, and the feeling was amazing. He wanted to kiss her again—very, very badly—but she was in full martial arts mode. She was *sensei* to his pupil and she was serious.

They had an hour during which he learned almost more than in the entire time the military had devoted to teaching hand-to-hand combat. And at the end he still didn't know a fraction of what this woman could do.

* * *

Karate was fun.

Dressmakers were scary.

The appointment was for two. Showered in the lavish gymnasium bathrooms, dressed again and with make-up newly applied, she should be ready for anything.

She wasn't.

Henri had come to find them. Raoul had left her for his own fittings and Henri had escorted her to a massive bedchamber on the second floor.

He swung the door wide and four women were waiting for her, all in black, all with faces carefully impassive.

'You'll take care of Miss Tremaine,' Henri said.

'Of course,' the oldest woman said smoothly, and closed the door on Henri and turned to appraise Claire.

She was a woman whose age was impossible to guess—slim, elegant, timeless. She also seemed deeply intimidating. Her gaze was surely a dressmaker's appraisal—nothing more. Claire shouldn't take it personally. But it was hard not to as every inch of her body was assessed and while the other three women stood back, silent, probably doing the same thing.

'Excellent,' the woman said at last. 'I'm Louise Dupont. These women are Marie, Belle and Fleur. Our job is to provide you with whatever you need for the grand ball and for the preceding official engagements which we're informed you're invited to attend. Belle has a list of the requirements. Would you like to tell us your ideas first, so we have an idea where we're going?'

'Simple.' It was as much as Claire could do to get the word out. 'I'm not royal, and I'm not accustomed to such events. If I could, I'd wear a little black dress...'

'A little black dress to a royal ball...?' Louise's expressionless face almost showed a flinch, and the women behind her gasped.

'I know I can't do that, but I'd like something that won't make me stand out.'

Certainly, *mademoiselle*,' Louise said woodenly, and swathes of cloth produced, and sketches, and a part of Claire was thinking, *What a coward.*

Among the swathes of cloth were brocades, sequins, tulle, lace of every description. But sense was sense. She chose beige for one of the anniversary dinners and a soft green for the other. Matching accessories. Deeply conservative. Then the ball dress...

'I really can't have black?'

'Their Majesties would consider it an insult,' Louise told her, and so Claire fingered the silver tulle for just a moment and then chose a muted sensible navy in a simple sheath design.

It will look elegant, she told herself, and the way the women set about fitting the cloth to her figure she knew it would.

And then Raoul arrived. One of the women answered the door to his tap. Whatever he'd tried on, he'd tried on fast. He was back in his casual trousers and open-necked shirt, but he stood in the doorway looking every inch a prince. He stared at the pinned sheath of navy cloth covering Claire and groaned.

'I *knew* it. Get it off.'

'I beg your pardon?' Louise turned and saw who it was, but her attitude hardly changed when she did. 'I beg your pardon—Your Highness.'

'Do you really think that's suitable for a royal ball?'

'It's what Miss Tremaine wishes.'

'Miss Tremaine wishes for the fairytale—don't you, Miss Tremaine?' He shook his head in exasperation. 'Louise, Miss Tremaine is returning to Australia after the ball, to life as a country lawyer. This ball is a ball to be remembered all her life.'

He strode across to where the remaining bolts of fabric lay and lifted some white lace shot with silver.

'This, I think. Something amazing, Louise. Something that makes the world look at Claire and know her for the beauty she is. She'll be wearing my mother's tiara…'

'Raoul!' She should have used his formal title but she was too gobsmacked. 'I don't want to stand out. Plain is good—and I'm not wearing a tiara.'

'You saved my life. If that's not a reason to lend you my mother's tiara I don't know what is. She'd be proud to have you wear it. You need a dress to match. Something magnificent, Louise. Something fairytale.'

'Would you like us to set up screens so you can supervise?'

'No!' Claire retorted.

Raoul grinned. 'What? No screens?'

'Go away!'

The women stared at her in astonishment—a commoner giving orders to royalty?—but Raoul was still smiling.

'Only if you promise to indulge in the fairytale. The full fantasy, Claire. Remember what Henri said? Have fun. Louise, can you do fairytale?'

'Certainly, Your Highness,' Louise told him, sounding intrigued.

'Then fairytale it is,' Raoul told her. 'Get rid of that navy blue.'

'Raoul…'

'I'm leaving,' he said, still smiling at her, and his smile was enough to have every woman in the room trying to hide a gasp. 'But you *will* have fun.'

'I will have fun,' she said grimly.

'That's my brave Claire. Go for it.'

And in the end she did have fun. Raoul left and she had two choices—she could try and incorporate a bit of bling into her image of plain or she could go for it.

With the women's blatant encouragement she went for it.

'I *do* like a bit of fairytale,' Louise admitted, letting her dour exterior drop.

Raoul had suggested the white lace shot with silver, and after a little thought that was what Louise recommended. The design she suggested was a gown of true princess splendour, with a low-cut sweetheart neckline and tiny slivers of silver just off the shoulders to hold the bodice in place. A vast skirt billowed and shimmered from a cinched waist, and a soft satin underskirt of the palest blue made the whole dress seem to light up.

That was the vision. For now it was only draped fabric, held together with pins, but Claire gazed at herself in the mirror and thought, *What am I doing here?*

She needed to ground herself. She needed to find Rocky and go home, she told herself as more and more of the shimmering silver was applied. To Australia. This fairytale was sucking her further and further in.

But she couldn't leave until after the ball.

At last the interminable measuring was done. 'You'll do our Prince proud,' Louise told her, permitting herself a tiny smile, and Claire tugged on her jeans and blouse as fast as she could and wondered how her presence could possibly do anyone proud. She felt a fraud.

Raoul was in the hallway, calmly reading, clearly waiting for her. He had Rocky on his knee. Rocky bounced across to greet her with canine delight and Raoul smiled—and she was in so much trouble.

'Hungry?' he asked. 'Picnic in the grounds?'

'Raoul, I should…'

'There's a whole lot of *I shoulds* waiting for us in the wings,' he said gently. 'For now, though, let's put them aside and focus on the *I wills*.'

CHAPTER TEN

RAOUL DIDN'T RETURN to her apartment that night, and neither did she stay in the palace. It had been a risk for one night; another night would be pushing things past reasonable limits if they were to keep the media treating their relationship as platonic. As they must.

Claire slept fitfully in her sparse apartment. She woke early, eager to throw herself back into work, which was far less confusing than being with Raoul. She was due to meet the head of Raoul's fledgling social services department. She drank coffee and read her notes from the previous week, trying to block out the fantasy of the weekend. Then, still with time before the car came to collect her, she retrieved the newspapers Raoul had organised to have delivered to her door.

She opened the first one and froze.

The page was entirely taken up with a photograph. Claire and Raoul, underneath the chandelier. The moment their waltz had ended. That kiss. The photograph had been blown up to the extent that the images were grainy, but there was no mistaking the passion.

This was no mere kiss. This was a kiss between

two lovers. This was a man and a woman who were deeply in love.

She gasped and backed into the hallway, as if burned, dropping the paper on the floor. She stared down at it in horror.

The headline…

Roturière Australienne Pièges Notre Prince.
Commoner Australian Traps Our Prince.

Scarcely breathing, she picked it up again.

The first article she read had been hurriedly but deeply researched.

When she'd first arrived in Marétal the press had given their readers a brief background of the woman who'd rescued their Prince.

Lawyer taking time out from successful career to caretake an island…

It had sounded vaguely romantic, and the description had been superficial.

There was nothing superficial about *this*. Overnight someone had been in touch with an Australian journalist, who must have travelled fast to the tiny Outback town of Kunamungle. There was an exposé of her childhood poverty and scandal, even a nasty jibe from the publican—*'She always thought she was better than us—she was dragged up in the gutter but ambition was her middle name…'*

More coming! the article promised, and Claire thought of the fraud allegations and what might come out—what *would* come out—and she felt ill.

This was sensationalist journalism and it cheapened everything. She felt smutty and used and infinitely weary.

She flicked to the next paper.

Prince Désire Paysanne...
Prince Desires Peasant.

The phone rang. It was Raoul. He spoke, but she couldn't make herself reply. She leant against the wall, feeling she needed its support. The papers were limp in her hands. She dropped them again and felt as if she wanted to drop herself.

'Claire, talk to me.'

'There's nothing to say,' she whispered. 'I knew this would happen. So did you.'

'I need to see you.' He groaned. 'But I can't. The media have staked out the palace gates. I'll be followed if I come to you and it'll make things worse.' He paused. 'Unless you want to face them down together?'

Together? With all that implied? 'No!'

Somehow she hauled herself together. She was here to do a job and she would do it.

'I have an appointment with the head of your social services department in half an hour,' she told him. 'In this precinct. I imagine the media can't get in here?'

'They can't. You'll still do that?'

'I promised,' she whispered. 'It's what I came here for.'

'You came here for so much more.'

'No,' she said, and anger came to her aid now—fury plain and simple. 'I didn't. I agreed to take on a job. If I go home now then your papers will say that every single thing they've printed is true. That I came here to trap you…'

'We both know that's a lie.'

'I bet that's what they said about Cinderella.'

'We're not basing our relationship on a fairytale.'

'You said it,' she said wearily. 'Raoul, it's impossible. This is real life. We had…we *could* have had…something amazing…but amazing doesn't solve real-life problems. You know I'm not good enough for you.'

And he swore—an expletive so strong she almost dropped the phone.

'Um…' she said at last. 'My translation isn't that good.'

'Claire, I *will* see you.'

'No,' she told him. 'It does neither of us any good.'

'You did promise you'd come to the ball.'

She fell silent then. The ball… She *had* promised. And there was the dress. And there was Raoul. And he'd be in his gorgeous regimental uniform.

Cinderella had *her* midnight, she thought rue-fully. Maybe she, too, could have her ball and her midnight. There'd be no glass slipper afterwards, because happy-ever-after only happened in fairy-tales, but the ball would be something she could remember all her life.

She shouldn't. The sensible part of her brain was screaming at her: *Don't, don't, don't!*

But there was still another part of her—the part that remembered Raoul holding her in the waltz, the part that remembered a dress of shimmering silver, the part that knew for the rest of her life she'd re-member one night…

And she had to finish what she'd come here to do. She'd do her work, she'd have her ball and she'd go home.

'Okay,' she whispered.

'Okay, what? Claire…'

'I will come to the ball,' she told him. 'As long as…as long as you don't attempt to see me before then. I won't come to the receptions. Just the ball. And I'll finish the work I'm here to do this week so I can go home straight afterwards.'

'It doesn't make any kind of sense'

'It does,' she said sadly. 'It makes all kinds of sense. It's anything else that's just plain lunacy.'

Raoul read the papers from cover to cover.

They were tearing Claire to pieces. No mercy…

This woman wasn't good enough to be the future Queen. The papers said so.

A fury was building inside him—a rage so cold, so hard, that it was all he could do not to smash things. The palace was full of excellent things to smash. Priceless china, artwork that still had the power to take his breath away, precious carpets and furnishings...

Right now he wanted to put a match to the lot of it and watch it burn.

Instead he forced himself to keep reading as he knew that Claire, when her work for the day was done, would read.

Together they could face them all down, he thought. This wasn't insurmountable. In time they'd see...

But she wouldn't let that happen. He knew that with a dull, unrelenting certainty. Claire's self-image had been battered from birth, and the ghastly Felicity and her cronies had smashed it to nothing. He knew how wonderful she was, but she'd never let herself believe it. She'd be miserable here, knowing everyone was looking down at her. Her self-image wouldn't let her go past it.

The whole situation was impossible. He slammed his fist down on his desk, causing his coffee to jump and topple and spill onto the priceless Persian rug.

Excellent. A good start.

There was a faint knock on the door.

'Come in,' he snapped, and Henri was at the door, looking grave.

'I am so sorry, Your Highness,' he told him.

'So am I.' He hesitated, and then thought, *Why not say it like it is?* 'The paper's right. I love her.'

Henri stilled. 'Truly?'

'What do *you* think?'

'This criticism will pass.'

'She doesn't think she's good enough, but she's better than all of us put together. What am I going to do? I can't demand she stay. I can't insist she subject herself to this sort of filth.' He picked up the top newspaper and tossed it down onto the pool of spilled coffee.

'She'd like to learn to ride,' Henri said weakly. 'Maybe you could ask her to come here for a lesson.'

'You think that would be an enticement for her to stay?'

'I…no.'

The two men stared at each other for a long moment. Raoul didn't even try to hide his pain. This man had known him since childhood. It was no use trying to hide.

'She must be really special,' Henri said at last.

'She saved my life,' Raoul said simply. He stared down at the spilled coffee and his mouth twisted. 'She saved *me*.'

'So how can you save her back?'

Raoul shrugged. 'I know the answer to that. I need to let her go.'

'There must be another way.'

'If you can think of one…' He lifted the newspaper he'd tossed and screwed it up. 'If you think the media will quit with this… It's relentless.'

'I'm so sorry,' Henri said gently. 'You know, the palace could put out a rebuttal…'

'Everything they say is true. They're crucifying her for things she had no hand in. They're crucifying her for her birth.'

'Are you thinking of marrying her?' Henri asked. 'Are you really thinking she's worthy of the throne?'

The question made Raoul pause. He thought of the years of isolation, of the armour he'd built around himself. He thought of his relentless quest not to need people. Not to love.

He thought of Claire.

'Are you really thinking she's worthy of the throne?'

She surely was. Of course she was. And then he thought of the throne without Claire and he was suddenly face to face with what he must have known for weeks.

'Of course I am,' he said bleakly. 'She's the woman I need beside me for the rest of my life.'

'Will she agree?'

'No,' he said bleakly. 'She won't, and I don't blame her.'

Claire spent the week working harder than she'd worked in her life. She'd been working to a plan and now she simply continued with the plan—except she worked faster.

She was interviewing as many of the country's movers and shakers in the justice system as she could. She was also talking to the police, prison officers, parole officers, small-time lawyers who worked at the fringe of the system—and to people who'd found themselves in court themselves. People who'd failed to find legal help when they'd needed it most. People whom legal assistance was designed to help.

As an outsider she could never have done this work alone, but Raoul had set it up for her. The people he and his staff had chosen for her to talk to were extraordinary, and to her relief almost none of them had backed out of the interviews because of the photograph and the lurid exposé of her past.

'I thought you wouldn't be here,' a lawyer she'd talked to that first morning had said. 'The papers say your legal work is just a smokescreen for you staying with the Prince.'

'It's not. My legal work is the reason His Highness persuaded me to come.'

'So you and the Prince…?' he'd probed, and she'd managed to smile.

'Legal work is dull. A woman has a right to a little fun on the side,' she'd told him, somehow managing to smile.

He'd stared at her in astonishment and then he'd laughed, and they'd got on with their interview.

So that was how she was managing it—laughing it off as best she could as a bit of fun, pretending it had nothing to do with her work and ignoring Raoul.

He still rang every night, and she answered his calls. She talked determinedly about the work she was doing—there was so much that could be done for his country and her report would be comprehensive—but she refused to talk about anything personal.

'Personal's a mistake,' she told him when he pressed her. 'You know that. And who knows who's listening in on this conversation?'

'No one is.'

'You can't be sure.'

'Claire…'

'I'll come to the ball and then I'm out of here,' she told him. 'My work will be done by then.'

'You know I want you to stay.'

'And it's totally unsuitable that I stay. Raoul, find yourself a princess. I'm just Claire.'

And each night she disconnected from his call with a firmness she didn't feel. She punched the pillows into the small hours and even made them a bit soggy, but there was no way she was relenting.

She had to do what she had to do and then leave.

Raoul also had to do what *he* had to do. As the week went on he became more and more sure that his decision was the right one. He needed her.

Need…

The knowledge made him feel exposed as he'd never been exposed before. It was terrifying and it was exhilarating and it was inarguable.

He'd lost his parents when he was so young he barely remembered them. His grandparents had been kind, but remote. He'd been raised by servants and then he'd found himself in the army—a place where teamwork was valued but individual emotional strength was everything.

He'd learned to be a loner. He'd thought he could be a loner all his life.

He'd been wrong, and the knowledge left him with no choice. Meeting Claire had made something inside him break and it couldn't be repaired.

A part of him said that was weak, but there was nothing he could do about it. Rejecting her felt like tearing himself apart.

He'd faced the worst of conflicts in the Middle East, but he'd joined the army for a reason. He'd spent a solitary childhood when life had seemed bleak to the point of misery. He thought of that solitude now. He had thought he'd trained himself to accept it.

He hadn't.

Two days before the ball he went to see his grandparents. Their discussion was intense, personal, a far cry from their usual formality, but at the end he knew his decision was the right one.

The King had said little, just looked grave.

The Queen had been appalled. 'You *can't*.'

'I might not be able to but I intend to try. Grand-mama, it's the only way I can stay sane.'

'She's not worth it. A commoner...'

'She's worth it.'

'Raoul, think of what you're risking,' she'd wailed, and he'd shaken his head.

'I think of what I'm gaining, Grandmama. We can do this if we work together.'

'You're not giving us a choice.'

'No,' he'd said, and he had glanced at the side table where the morning newspapers were, full of even more vituperative stories about his Claire. 'No, I'm not. The country's condemned Claire and in doing so it's refused the best thing that's ever happened to it. And it's rejected the best thing that's ever happened to *me*.'

Cinderella had her coach at midnight. Claire had her plane tickets. Her flight back to Australia was booked for early in the morning after the ball.

'It's the same thing, except I won't be leaving any glass slippers behind,' she told herself.

She was standing before the full-length mirror in her apartment, staring at herself in awe. She'd been invited to dress at the palace but she'd refused, so Henri had organised a dresser, a hairstylist and a make-up artist to come to her. She therefore had three women fussing about her. A chauffeur was standing by with a limousine in the courtyard.

For this night she was deemed royalty.

One night before the rest of her life…

She stood in front of the mirror and knew exactly how Cinderella had felt.

This wasn't her. This was truly a princess.

Her reflection left her feeling stunned. She looked taller, slimmer, glowing. She looked regal. Her curls were loosely caught up, deceptively casual, so they framed her face, tumbled artfully to her shoulders. They were caught back within a glittering tiara so some curls hid the diamonds and some diamonds sparkled through.

The tiara alone had made her catch her breath in wonder, but there was also a matching necklet and earrings.

'They haven't been worn since the Prince's mother died,' the dresser said now, sniffing faintly in disapproval. 'I'm astonished that he thinks it's suitable to bring them out today.'

And there it was—the whole reason this wouldn't work. This woman had read the tabloids. She knew just how unsuitable Claire was.

'I guess it's a final thank-you gift before I go home,' Claire said, managing to keep her voice light, as she'd fought to keep it light all week. 'And it *is* just a loan…'

'But for him to lend it…'

'Well, *I* think it's lovely,' the hairstylist said stoutly. 'Perfect. And I loved the picture of you and His Highness in the paper, miss. So romantic. Wouldn't it be lovely if it was real?'

'I think I might regret it if it was real,' Claire managed. 'Do I absolutely need to wear this corset?'

'Hourglass figures need hourglass corsets,' the dresser snapped. 'The women I normally dress don't complain. You must make sacrifices for a decent figure'

'You have a lovely figure already,' the hairstylist declared. 'Don't listen to her, miss.'

And Claire wasn't listening. This week had been all about not listening.

She stared once more into the mirror at the sparkling vision in silver and white, at the way her skirts shimmered and swung, at the beautiful white slippers—not glass!—peeping from under her skirts. At her hair, which had surely never been lovelier. At the carefully applied make-up, which made it look as if she was wearing no make-up at all and yet made her complexion glow. At the diamonds and the sparkle and everything in life which didn't represent Claire Tremaine.

'Okay,' she whispered. 'Bring on my pumpkin.'

'Your car's ready, miss,' the stylist breathed. 'Oh, miss, you'll break your Prince's heart tonight.'

'He's not my Prince,' Claire told her, gathering her skirts and her courage. 'He's never been my Prince and he never will be.'

* * *

The ball was an hour old when Claire arrived.

Raoul was half afraid that she'd got cold feet and wouldn't show at all, but at this late stage there was little he could do about it. As heir to the throne he opened the ball with a waltz with the Queen of a neighbouring country. Then there were others he needed to dance with. He had obligations to fulfil and there was no way he could disappear quietly to phone her.

All he could do was dance on with the list of notables Henri had told him were compulsory, and hope that she'd find the courage to come.

Finally he was rewarded when a stir from the entrance announced her arrival.

'Miss Claire Tremaine,' the footman announced in stentorian tones.

The ball was well under way. The announcement of new arrivals had become a muted background to the night—no one was listening—but somehow all ears caught this.

The attention of the entire ballroom seemed to swing to Claire.

She was stunning. Breathtaking.

Henri must have orchestrated this late entrance, he thought. Henri was in charge of Claire's travel arrangements. Raoul wouldn't put it past him to have staged Claire's entrance so she had maximum attention.

As she did. She stood in the entrance looking

slightly unsure—no, make that *very* unsure. She looked so lovely the entire ballroom seemed to hold its breath.

His grandmother was by his side and her hand clutched his arm. 'You don't need to go straight to her,' she hissed. 'The way she looks…others will dance with her. This is nonsense, Raoul. See sense.'

'I *am* seeing sense,' he told her. 'Grandmama, you know what I must do.'

'Not tonight,' she urged. 'You need to accompany us onto the dais for the speech. You need to be seen as royal. Stay with us.'

'Only if you acknowledge Claire.'

'I'll acknowledge her as the woman who saved your life, nothing more.'

'Then I'll be in the crowd, watching. If you expect me to be an onlooker, so be it. But meanwhile…' He gently disengaged her arm. 'Meanwhile I need to welcome the woman I love.'

It might as well have been a fairytale. For as she stood, uncertain, alone, Raoul made his way through the crowd and quite literally took her breath away.

The ballroom itself was enough to take her breath away. It was transformed by the lights from the great chandelier, by a thousand flowers, by an orchestra playing music that soared, by the throng of nobility in attire that was truly splendid.

But the most splendid of all was Raoul.

He was truly a prince of dreams. He was in full

royal regalia, a superbly cut suit with a wide blue sash, medals, epaulettes, glittering adornments of royal blood and military might.

His jet-black hair was immaculate. His height, his build, his dress—he looked every inch a prince at the peak of his power. He was the total antithesis of the man she'd helped from the water.

He was magnificent.

He was smiling as he broke through the throng, and he held his hand out to her well before he reached her.

'Miss Tremaine,' he said as he reached her. 'You are very welcome.'

And her response was something that stunned even herself. She sank into a curtsy—a full gesture that she hadn't known how to make until she'd done it.

He took her hand and raised her fingers to his lips, his eyes dancing with laughter.

'What have I done to deserve this?'

'I've watched too many romantic movies,' she told him. 'In this outfit nothing else seems appropriate.'

'Claire, stay...' The laughter died and his voice was low and urgent.

'For tonight,' she whispered. 'For now.'

If tonight was all he had then he intended to use it. How to hold this woman in his arms, how to dance with her, how to feel her melting against him and know that she willed it to end?

But he knew why. All around them were eyes raised, looks askance, the occasional snigger, the odd snort of outrage. *This* was the woman who would steal their royal Prince. He knew Claire could feel it, and there was nothing he could do but hold her and know there must be a future for them.

A future at a cost…

But he couldn't think of that tonight. He couldn't think of anything but the woman in his arms.

As they danced the titters and the whispers fell away. He held her and her beautiful gown swirled against his legs, and her breasts moulded to his chest and he felt…

He felt as if he was flying.

She loved him. How could she let him hold her like this and know that she had to leave? If she let herself think past midnight then her mind simply shut down.

All she was capable of was dancing with the man she loved. Of holding him to her.

Of loving…

Only, of course, the night wasn't all about dancing. There were formalities scheduled. After the next set the King and Queen were to make their anniversary speech. And as they made their way to the stage they paused by the couple in the midst of the dance floor.

'You should stand by us, Raoul,' the Queen told

him, but she said it in the tone of one who knew she was already beaten.

'You know my decision,' Raoul said softly. 'I stand by Claire.'

'Raoul—go,' Claire told him.

'Will we come to the stage as a couple, Grand-mama?' Raoul asked, but the Queen shook her head.

'No! This is *not* what I planned.'

'I'm staying here,' Raoul told her.

'Then come onto the stage with us yourself, young woman,' the King told Claire unexpectedly, suddenly urgent. As if he'd somehow emerged from his books and was seeing Raoul's firmness for what it was. 'This country's treating you shabbily and I won't have it.' He put a hand on her arm. 'Come with us. Please.'

'As a couple,' Raoul said.

'No!' The Queen was vehement.

'Then come to assist an old man onto the stage,' the King told Claire. 'Raoul, assist your grand-mother.' And he took Claire's arm and held it.

So in the end there was no choice. They made their way to the stage, but not as a couple. The King was escorted up first, leaning heavily on Claire as if he did indeed need her help.

Raoul escorted his grandmother up the stairs as well. But then, as she made to tug at him, to stand beside her on the far side of the stage from Claire, he shook his head.

'Claire, our place isn't here.'

The noise from the ballroom had faded. Attention was riveted on the stage. To reach Raoul, to leave the stage, Claire would have to walk right in front of both King and Queen.

Raoul was on the far side of the stage, waiting for her to return to him. She sent him an almost imperceptible shake of her head and backed into the wings. The curtains hid her.

This was her rightful place, she thought. Out of sight. She was in the wings with the workers, with the people handling the curtains, the workers associated with the orchestra.

Where she belonged.

She leaned heavily against the nearest wall and hoped Raoul wouldn't follow.

Fantasy was over. The King was preparing to speak.

Somewhere below was Raoul. He needed to listen to his grandparents' speech but she didn't need to be beside him.

She couldn't need him at all.

If there was one thing King Marcus had been known for during his long reign it was his long speeches—and he didn't disappoint now. He'd prepared a very meaningful, very erudite, very lengthy speech and the crowd settled down to listen. This was their King. The country was fond enough of their Queen, but King Marcus was seldom seen in public and they were prepared to indulge him when he was.

After a moment's hesitation Raoul backed away from the stage, stepping down into the main hall. He didn't want any attention to play on him. After all, this was his grandparents' night, and he even found it within him to be grateful that Claire had backed into the wings, out of sight. The focus was on his grandparents—as it should be. The time for him to claim Claire would follow.

Around him the guests were listening with polite attention, laughing when the King meant them to laugh, applauding when it was appropriate. The men and woman in the orchestra behind the King were all attentive too. They were giving this pair of beloved monarchs their due.

He had a sudden vision of himself and Claire in fifty years, doing the same thing.

It wasn't going to happen.

He glanced at his grandmother and found she was staring straight at him. He winced and turned his attention elsewhere. To the orchestra on the raised platform behind the royals. Men and women in demure black, riveted to the King's words.

Except one. A young man seated behind the drums. The man seemed to be searching the crowd. Looking for someone?

His attention caught, Raoul followed his gaze and saw the man's eyes meet one of the guests. A man in his mid-forties was standing not far from Raoul. He was formally dressed, as a foreign diplomat, and he was standing alone. There was nothing to make him stand out from so many similar guests.

But the man was watching the drummer, not the King, and as the drummer's gaze met his he gave his head an almost imperceptible nod. Then casually—oh, so casually—he reached down as if to adjust his shoelace.

And then he straightened, his arm outstretched…

A glint of metal…

Years of military training had made Raoul's reactions lightning-fast. Act first—ask questions later. That was the training instilled for when lives were at stake.

Raoul, ten feet from the man in question, dived like lightning and brought him down in a tackle that pinned him to the floor.

The pistol in the man's hand discharged—straight into the polished floor. But that wasn't the only threat. He knew it wasn't. He held the man, pinned him down hard, and looked desperately up at the stage as he yelled. 'Security! Drummer on stage!'

And as the dark-suited security officers streamed in from the foyer, where they'd been banished, he was remembering a letter. It had been pointed out to him by Henri. It had been addressed to the Queen…

If you don't follow our orders we'll kill the King and take you as our prisoner for ransom. You might as well pay the money now. It'll save you grief…

There'd been a similar threat—and a tragedy—in another country a couple of years back. Their security chief had been worried enough to talk to the Queen, asking permission to bolster his team. He'd wanted to increase the royal security presence within the ballroom.

'You can do what you want *after* the ball,' the Queen had said fretfully. 'I won't have my ball marred by a room full of bodyguards.'

He'd then shared his concerns with Henri, who'd come to Raoul. 'Please...talk to your grandmother,' Henri had told him, and Raoul had. But with no success.

'You're not in charge yet,' the Queen had told him. 'This is *our* ball. You won't bring a woman of our choice. We won't have your bodyguards.'

'They're not *my* bodyguards, Grandmama. They're yours—to keep you safe.'

'There is no threat in *my* kingdom.'

But of course there was—and it was here. It was real. A diplomat wouldn't have faced a body-search. He'd have been able to conceal a gun.

We'll kill the King and take you as our prisoner...

There were two threats here, and he'd only disarmed one.

'The drummer on stage!' he yelled again to the men approaching.

'Nobody move!' a voice shouted out—icy, cold, vicious.

And Raoul twisted and stared up at the stage.

The drummer had launched himself in from the wings and grabbed the Queen. She'd been standing beside the dais while her husband spoke. The man dragged her back towards the wings, and at her throat he held a vicious, stiletto-type knife that looked as if it might have been concealed in a drumstick.

And Claire was there as well. At the sound of the gunshot and Raoul's sharp command she'd edged out from the wings.

She was right behind the drummer.

The three of them might well have been alone on stage. The men and women in the orchestra were slightly removed from the main players. The King was standing stunned on his dais.

There was the Queen and her assailant—and Claire.

The drummer was hauling the Queen further back, and as he did so he glanced behind him. He saw Claire.

He flicked her a glance that took in the swirl of her amazing skirts, her low-cut neckline and the gorgeous tiara set in beautifully coiffured curls. His glance was contemptuous—a momentary summing-up that said she was nothing of importance.

She was the dirt the media had been speaking of. She was something to be safely ignored.

He had his knife to Queen Alicia's throat and was tugging her backwards.

For the moment Queen Alicia was refusing to move, digging in her toes, dragging passively, surprisingly fierce for someone so elderly. 'Let me go,' she ordered, in a voice as imperious as her regalia.

'Shut up!' the drummer snarled, and then as the appalled hiss from the ballroom faded to stunned silence he raised his voice. 'One move from anyone and I'll kill your Queen. If she's so precious, stay where you are. She's coming with me. And *you…*' He turned to Raoul. 'Let my friend go.'

Raoul was at the far end of the ballroom. He was with the security forces. They had the diplomat in their grip.

Raoul had the gun in his hand. The sound of its explosion was still reverberating through the horrified throng. He raised the gun and then lowered it, watched helplessly as the security officers did the same.

The drummer was holding the Queen hard in front of him. To shoot risked killing her. There was nothing he could do.

'Let him go!' the drummer snarled again, talking directly to Raoul. 'Now!'

There was no choice. Raoul gave a nod and the security officers let the man go. The man started to move up through the crowded ballroom, shoving stunned aristocracy aside.

And Claire's mind was racing. In a minute she'd have two of them on the dais, she thought. In a minute they'd have the Queen outside, in their hold. Raoul was powerless.

A minute…

She needed a second.

And the voice of her *sensei*…

She glanced out at Raoul, one sweeping glance in which their eyes met for just a fraction of a second but the message she gave him was powerful.

And then she had to ignore him. She had to move. *Now.*

She kicked off her ridiculously high, ridiculously beautiful shoes and in almost the same movement lifted her voluminous skirts high. She raised her gartered knee as high as she could and with the heel of her bare foot slammed a *yoko geri* side-kick with lethal force into the back of the assailant's knee.

She'd only ever done this in training. She'd only ever known it as practice, and she'd certainly never done it while dressed in a corset and ballgown.

'Do this and you'll rip ligaments, or worse,' her *sensei* had told her. 'The first rule of Karate is not to be present. Where there is trouble, you are not. But if you're ever trapped in a life-or-death situation this will cause extreme pain and do enough serious damage to give you time to escape.'

And there was no doubt that was exactly what she'd done. The guy screamed and started to drop.

There was still the knife. He could kill the Queen if he dragged her with him, but years of training, years of knowledge and practice were flooding to her aid. What followed was almost a reflex action. Even as the guy buckled she had his knife arm by the wrist and was pulling it back, her other hand pressed against his elbow, pushing forward. She pressed hard with both hands and the guy screeched in pain.

'Drop it,' she bit out as his knees hit the floor.

Queen Alicia was crumbling with them, unbalanced by the change of pressure. The combined mass of royal skirts was making the entire scene surreal—where were crisp karate uniforms when she needed them?—but she was totally focused on her assailant.

The guy's hand jerked, still holding the knife. 'You slut…'

'I'm not a slut,' she said calmly. 'But I *am* a Third Dan Karate Black Belt. Drop the knife or I'll break your arm.' And she applied more pressure. Not so much as required to break it—at least she didn't think so—but enough to have him screaming again.

Enough to have the knife clattering harmlessly to the floor.

She fielded it and kicked it under Alicia's skirts—because who knew who was out there in the ballroom if she kicked it off the dais?

And she kept on holding the guy's arm, pushing him flat to the floor, with his arm still held behind him, because she didn't know if the knife was all he had. And then she didn't have to hold him, because Raoul was leaping up onto the dais with her.

She glanced out over the ballroom and realised he'd got her silent message. The security officers had moved, obviously at Raoul's command. The man he'd had to release had been grasped again.

They had them.

Security was suddenly everywhere. Control was theirs.

The guy was underneath her. The last threat. And Raoul was with her.

It was over.

CHAPTER ELEVEN

AT FIVE THE next morning Claire boarded her plane.

Why not?

There was no reason why not. The ball had ended in disarray. The security team hadn't been prepared to let it continue. Who knew what else had been planned?

The guests had dispersed, vetted as they left, their credentials finally minutely inspected.

The Queen had collapsed in hysterics. Raoul had been taken up with security concerns, with coping with the ruffled feathers and nerves of the invited dignitaries, with the calming of his distraught grandparents.

Apart from one brief, hard embrace when they'd realised the danger was past, Claire hadn't seen him. She'd been whisked outside by the security people and Henri had appeared at her side and asked her if she'd like to use a salon in the palace to wait for Raoul.

'I'd like to go home,' she'd told him, and he'd nodded gravely and organised a car to take her back to her apartment. Because that was what he thought home meant.

An hour later a slim figure in jeans and a wind-cheater had slipped out of her apartment, carrying her own baggage to the taxi she herself had arranged.

And now she was on the plane, staring fixedly forward while she waited for take-off. White-faced but determined. What a way to end it. Maybe she should have waited, but her ticket was for this morning and there was no point. What had to be said had been said.

Marétal to London. London to Sydney. In twenty-four hours she'd be back in the apartment she hadn't been near for almost six months.

She had work to do—she'd come to Marétal on a contract and she'd fulfil her obligations. The next few months would be busy. But she wouldn't return to Marétal. Her report would be emailed. Raoul and his staff could use it or not.

She felt ill.

'Orange juice?' A steward was moving down the aisle, offering refreshments. 'I'm sorry, but there's a slight delay in take-off. It shouldn't be more than half an hour.'

She closed her eyes. Half an hour. The beginning of the rest of her life.

Raoul. How could she leave him?

How could she not?

She should be exhausted. She should sleep. But of course sleep was nowhere. She was still wired, still filled with adrenalin, still seeing Raoul heading towards the stage to help her. Still seeing the fear on his face.

He loved her. She knew he loved her. And to be loved by such a man…

Such an impossible man.

There was a stir among the passengers and she opened her eyes and glanced out of the window. There were two dark limousines, their windows tinted to anonymity in the dawn light, driving onto the tarmac. They stopped and a security contingent emerged from the second car—suited men, armed, dangerous.

Where had they been last night?

And then the door of the first car opened and out stepped…

Raoul.

Raoul in jeans and T-shirt, carrying a rough canvas duffel. Raoul looking every inch *not* a royal.

There was fierce talk between the men—remonstrance? But Raoul simply shook each man's hand and then turned and looked up at the plane.

She shrank back. If he was here to take her off the plane…

She wouldn't go. She couldn't.

She sat head down, scarcely daring to breathe, but nothing happened. She couldn't see the door from where she sat. There was a murmur of interest from the passengers forward of her and then nothing.

'Prepare for take-off…'

Nothing more was said. She ventured a peek out of the window. The cars were gone.

The plane turned its big nose ponderously out to the runway, the taxiing complete.

She closed her eyes as the plane gathered speed and then they were in the air.

Marétal was left behind.

'Would you like a facecloth?' An attendant was moving down the aisle, doing her normal thing, business as usual.

She offered the facecloth to Claire and Claire buried her face in it.

'Hi,' said a voice behind the attendant—a voice she knew so well. 'Do you think that when you're all washed up you can cope with a visitor?'

The seat next to hers was empty. Of course it was.

That couldn't just be a coincidence, she thought as Raoul sank down beside her, and amazingly she even found space to be indignant. The plane was almost full. How had he managed this?

He was royal. Being royal opened doors.

'Very nice,' Raoul said approvingly as he sank into the business class seat. 'I'm back in cattle class. I had to be ever so charming to the staff to be allowed up here.'

'You're in Economy?' As a first statement it was pretty dumb, but then dumb was how she was feeling right now.

'*Your* travel is funded by the Royal Family of Marétal,' he told her. 'I'm funded by me. And I'm unemployed. We unemployed people need to watch every cent.'

It was too much to take in. 'Why...why are you here?' she managed, and for answer he simply took her hand.

'You saved the life of the Queen of Marétal. Someone has to thank you. I got busy, and when I had time to look around you were gone.'

'I had a plane ticket.'

'So you did.' His hold on her hand tightened. 'As it happened, so did I.'

'You...?'

'You don't think I'd let you go all the way to Australia without me?'

'Of course I do,' she snapped. She was tired, confused, and starting to be angry. 'Raoul, this was never the plan. Go away.'

'It's a bit hard to go away now,' he said, peering out of the window to the night sky. They were now thousands of feet high. 'I believe I've burned my bridges. Henri's cleaning up the loose ends in Marétal. I'm here with you.'

'Henri...'

'He's good,' Raoul told her. 'He's the new administrator of the country. I'm unemployed.'

Unemployed...

He took her breath away. He was looking endearingly casual, in jeans and a tight T-shirt that showed every muscle his army life had toned. He was starting to look a bit unshaven. The difference between now and when she'd last seen him was extraordinary.

Unemployed?

'I've quit,' he told her, settling in. 'This is very nice indeed. How long do you think they'll let me sit here?'

'As long as you want. You're the Prince,' she snapped.

He shook his head. 'Nope. I need a new title. I've been Prince Raoul. I've been Lieutenant Colonel de Castelaise. Now I need to be just plain mister. Mr de Castelaise? That sounds wrong. *Monsieur?* Yes, but I intend to be an Aussie. Any suggestions?'

She had no suggestions at all. She could only stare. If she went back behind her facecloth again would he disappear? This felt surreal.

She was starting to feel as Cinders must have felt when her coach had turned back into a pumpkin. In the middle of the road surrounded by orange pulp. Stranded.

Hornswoggled.

'You can't...just resign,' she managed at last, and Raoul nodded, thoughtful.

'That's what I thought. I couldn't see how I could. But when it got closer to losing you I didn't see how I *couldn't.*'

'Your country needs you.' Her voice was scarcely a whisper.

'That's what I believed, too,' he told her. 'But over the last few weeks I've been looking hard at how our country's run and seeing things in a different light.'

'I don't understand.'

'I'm not sure I do either,' he told her. 'Not fully. But what I *do* know is that my grandfather wasn't born to rule. Yes, he was the heir to the throne, but his head was always in his books. His parents despaired of him. His country despaired of him. But then he did something amazing. He met and married my grandmother. She wasn't what you might call a commoner—she was Lady Alicia Todd—but she was just the daughter of a country squire and she had no pretensions to royalty. But she married my grandfather, she took up the reins of the country, and she's been a superb monarch. She's fading now. She's ceased to move with the times, but she's still awesome. She's still the Queen.'

'She needs help. You said yourself...'

'I know she does. But when I was thinking this through I wondered... All those years ago, what would my grandfather have done if someone had told him—as I believe many people did—that Alicia wasn't fit to be Queen? And the answer was obvious. He would have abdicated rather than lose her.'

'You're not threatening...?' Still she was having trouble getting her voice to work. 'You're not threatening to abdicate?'

'I haven't threatened anything,' he told her. 'I've left.'

'You've walked out?'

'Hey, I'm honourable,' he told her, sounding wounded. 'How could I just walk out?'

'You tell me. Words of one syllable,' she said, trying hard to glare. 'What have you done?'

'Moved the Crown into administration.' He thought about it for a moment and reconsidered. 'That's a three-syllable word. Thrown the reins to Henri? Henri's still two syllables, but he's the best I can do. This whole situation is the best I can do.'

'Raoul…'

'You see, Henri doesn't want it,' Raoul told her. 'In fact he's still trying to talk me out of it. But we're organising good people around him. It'll take time, and I will have to return to get things into final shape, but we'll make it work. We don't have a choice.'

'But you're *needed*,' she said, flabbergasted. 'Raoul, you know you are.'

'And I intend to stay hands-on,' he told her. 'I'll return every so often, for as long as they need me. If my grandfather's health declines further, then those visits might end up being long, but that's all they will be. Visits.'

'How can you *do* that? They need you all the time.'

'And there's the problem,' he told her. 'I need *you* all the time.'

That took her breath away. She wasn't sure how she could make herself breathe, much less talk, but somehow she must.

'Isn't that…?' She could hardly make herself say it, but it had to be said. 'Isn't that selfish? Your country needs you. Even on so short a visit I could see the difference you'd make.'

There was a moment's silence. His face set, and she knew suddenly that what he was proposing was no whim. What he was saying was the end of some bitter internal battle, and even now the outcome hurt.

'I could make a difference,' he agreed at last. 'I know I could. But, Claire, the more I see of you the more I know I couldn't.'

'I don't understand…'

'Last week, after that appalling photograph and the ensuing fuss, I went to see my grandparents,' he told her. 'I talked to both of them and I asked them honestly if they could have ruled for so long and for so well if they hadn't had each other. My grandfather, the King, was the first to answer and he was blunt. He said Alicia was his strength, and that he'd never have been able to do it alone. That's what I expected. But then my grandmother decided to be honest as well. She told me that, strong as she appeared, my grandfather was her spine. That without him she believed she'd collapse like a house of cards. That her love for him was what sustained her. And she conceded more. That royalty was a massive privilege but also a massive burden. And she said that, disapprove of you—*and* your dog—as she surely did, if I truly loved you then she understood. She'd fight me all the way to the altar—she would *not* support me marrying someone so patently un-suitable—but she understood.'

'Oh, Raoul…' Where was the facecloth when she needed it?

But Raoul had her fingers under her chin, forcing her gaze to meet his. 'So it's Henri,' he told her. 'It's Henri and our staff, and my grandparents, and me working from the sidelines. In time the country will become a democracy and they'll see they don't really need a monarch. We'll work something out. We must.'

'But *you*?' It was almost a wail. 'Raoul, it'll take years to make Marétal a democracy, and even then the monarchy could stay in place. You'd make a wonderful king.'

'Not without you.'

'That's crazy. I could never be royal. Your whole country thinks I'm a piece of dirt.'

'So my whole country can think we're *both* pieces of dirt,' he told her. 'I dare say they will when they wake up tomorrow. *Prince Absconds With the Love of His Life.* I hope that's the headline.'

'After the events at the ball it could be *Prince's Senses Blown to Pieces.*'

'The Prince's senses are indeed blown,' Raoul said.

He was still tilting her face, and his eyes were now smiling. His appalling decision to leave the succession was put aside. What mattered now was them.

'They've been blown apart by one green girl.

Claire, I'm coming to Australia with you, whether you will it or not. Where you go, I go. Your home is my home. I'm not exactly sure what I'll do yet—I'm thinking maybe a job in security? A bouncer at a pub? What do you think? Your career prospects are so much better than mine right now, but regardless...unemployed or not... Claire Tremaine, will you marry me?'

And there was the end of breathing. Who needed to breathe? Who could even *think* of breathing?

'I can't,' she managed at last. She was struggling between tears and laughter. 'Raoul, you know I can't.'

'Why not? Are you too good to marry a bouncer?'

'Raoul, you're a *prince*.'

'I can't be a prince without a princess. I thought I could. I was an idiot.'

'You can't throw it all away.'

'I already have. I booked this flight days ago, and then last night you showed me your *yoko geri* side-kick—that's what our security chief tells me it was—and any last niggles of doubt were gone. My brave girl. My heroine. My heart's yours, Claire Tremaine. I'm your faithful shadow. You can be a lawyer wherever you want and I'll be right there beside you.'

Then suddenly he paused, as if struck by inspiration.

'Wait. I have it. You and I could be a team. We

could train Rocky to be our killer attack dog. Attack Dog Security—how does that sound as a family business?'

'Right…'

'It *is* right, though, isn't it?' Laughter faded. Everything faded. 'Claire, I'd give up the world for you. Indeed, I don't have a choice—because you *are* my world. Marry me, my love, and somehow we'll make a future together.'

'Raoul…' But she couldn't say more.

He tugged her into his arms and kissed her and she let herself be kissed. She even melted into the kiss. But when the kiss drew to an end and she managed to tug away her eyes were still troubled.

'I don't know what to do,' she whispered.

'I do,' he told her. 'Marry me.'

'But the future…'

'Will fall into place. It must because it doesn't have a choice. Marry me, my love. My Claire. Please.'

And what was a woman to say to that, when Raoul was looking at her with such a look?

Heart on his sleeve… She'd heard the expression so many times…wearing your heart on your sleeve…and she'd thought nothing of it.

But it was true. Raoul was hanging his heart on his sleeve right now. He was caressing her with his eyes, loving her, wanting her.

What did the future hold for both of them? She

didn't know. But sitting beside him in the quiet of the plane, looking steadily into eyes that loved her, she knew she had only one answer to give.

'Yes, my love,' she whispered. 'Come what may, I guess…I'll marry you.'

They stopped to change to another flight in London, sat in the airport lounge and barely spoke. None of the passengers from the Marétal flight seemed to be going on to Australia, so no one knew them.

Claire leant on Raoul's chest and slept.

He sat and held her and felt his world shift and shift again. *What had he done?*

He'd set things up as best he could at home. Henri was in charge. With the army manoeuvres finished, the best of Marétal's army was home again, so Franz himself could investigate the aftermath of the events of the ball.

His grandparents had been devastated at his decision to leave, but at least they understood.

He was free to hold this woman forever.

But he wasn't quite free.

A niggle of doubt still troubled him. He knew sometimes that niggle would become a shout, but still… To take the throne without her… He'd self-destruct—he knew he would. These last weeks had become a tangle of introspection, of self-questioning, and in the end he'd come up with what he knew was the absolute truth. He wasn't a loner, and the throne was essentially one of the loneliest places in the world.

Was it weak to say he knew he'd self-destruct? A lifetime on the throne without Claire? He'd looked long and hard at himself and known he couldn't face it.

He loved her.

He held her in his arms while she slept. His chin rested on her hair. She was trusting in sleep, her mouth curved into a faint, loving smile. He had the woman he loved most in the world right here in his arms and nothing else could matter.

He'd do everything in his power to keep Marétal safe, to see it into a prosperous future, but he couldn't give up Claire. This woman was his and he was hers.

The future stretched ahead in all its uncertainty, but for now… He was with Claire and that was all that could matter.

She shouldn't let him do it. For Raoul to abdicate… for *her*…

He mustn't.

She knew he mustn't but she'd said yes.

How selfish was that?

It was impossible, and yet she couldn't let herself think of impossibility. Soon she'd wake up to reality, she thought as she lay nestled in Raoul's arms, half asleep.

Soon she'd wake up—but not yet. Please, not yet.

Sydney, Australia.

'We can't go to my apartment,' Claire had told him as they landed. 'Firstly it's a shoebox, and won't fit us both, and secondly I've sublet it. I…*we* need to find something else. I meant to go to a hostel…'

'Hostels mean dormitories,' he'd said, and had taken charge.

She woke up after a glorious twelve hours' sleep to find herself cocooned in Raoul's arms, sunlight streaming in through the windows of their hotel room and a view of Sydney Harbour that was truly breathtaking.

'So…so much for being unemployed,' she managed as Raoul stirred with her. 'Five-star luxury… We need to say goodbye to all this.'

'Not this morning, woman,' he growled, holding her to him. 'Not until I'm over jet lag—and I hear jet lag lasts a long time. And there's only one cure. Come here and I'll show you.'

And the spectre of unemployment went right out of the window as she turned within his arms and smiled at her beloved, and then melted as she surely must. *Oh, Raoul…*

They loved and loved, and for the moment the cares of the world were put firmly aside in their joy with each other.

But finally the world had to intrude—of course it did. Hunger had a habit of asserting itself even in the most fabulous of settings.

They made themselves decent—sort of—and ordered breakfast, and Claire gasped when she saw it.

'We can't do this. You've said you're an unemployed bouncer. Champagne for breakfast?'

'If I'm not mistaken you've just agreed to marry me. There are some occasions when even unemployed bouncers require the best.'

And who was arguing this morning? Just for today she could put doubts aside and drink her lovely champagne and eat her gorgeous croissants and look lovingly at this gorgeous prince-cum-bouncer as he finished his own croissant and reached lazily for the newspapers that had been delivered with the breakfast tray.

She watched his face change.

'What?' she said, and rose and went to stand beside him.

They were in the breakfast nook—a curved bay window overlooking the sparkling waters of Sydney Harbour. They were both dressed in the towelling robes provided by the hotel. It was the most beautiful, most intimate of settings—a breakfast to remember—and yet as she watched him she saw the dreamlike quality fall away and reality set in.

'Problems?'

'No,' he told her. 'It's just…I didn't think it'd make the news here. You're going to be hounded again.'

And there it was—a front-page spread—and once again she was in the centre. Claire in her Cinderella dress. Claire in the moments after Raoul had reached the stage, the attackers disarmed. Raoul leading her to safety. Raoul in his beautiful prince's clothes, his arm around her, curved in protection.

And the headlines…

Australian Woman Saves Queen…
Assassination Attempt Foiled…

'I might have known,' Raoul said. 'All media's parochial. Your press will have picked up that there was an Australian in the middle of it and gone with that angle. Claire, I'm sorry.'

'I can live with a few days' media attention,' she said, and managed a smile. 'Especially if we can stay here. Hunker down. Let the world forget us.'

'We might be able to manage that.' He tugged her down onto his knee. 'That's what you want? For the world to forget us?'

And she thought, *Did she?*

For herself? Definitely. Since when did publicity mean anything good? As a child she'd hated anyone looking at her. The taunts. The active discrimination against the child of a single mum…

Yes, she'd hated it and feared it. And the whole lawsuit thing had terrified her even more.

Raoul had had a lifetime of attention being trained on him. Surely he must hate it, too.

She knew he did, but now he was fetching his laptop from his bag, logging in to the internet.

'I need to see what the papers are saying at home,' he told her.

And she thought, *Home? Home is where?*

He was sitting on the bed and she went to join him. He put the laptop where they could both see.

There'd been two mornings in Marétal since they'd left. Two lots of newspapers.

The first newspapers they read were those published in the immediate aftermath of the drama. There were photographs of the white-faced King and Queen, dignified but clearly shaken. There were fuzzy photographs of the attackers being led away by Security. There were photographs of the King and Queen, and of Raoul and Claire.

Saved by Our Prince! the headline screamed, and Raoul winced.

'That's hardly fair.'

'You stopped him firing.'

'And if it wasn't for you the Queen would have been taken and held for ransom,' Raoul told her, and flicked through to the next day's headlines.

Which were different.

The reporters had had time to figure out the details of what had happened.

There was a photograph of Alicia with the knife at her throat, being hauled back towards the wings.

There was a photograph, slightly blurred, of a make-believe princess, her dress hiked up, her legs bare, her shoes kicked off. The moment her foot had come into contact with the assailant's knee. A second photograph of her grip on his arm.

The third photograph was of Raoul, launching himself onto the stage to help her hold.

And the headlines?

The Woman We Called Commoner...
The Princess We Need.

She didn't say anything. She simply sat as Raoul read out the stark article underneath.

Our Prince and the woman he loves saved our King and Queen. This woman we've condemned has done our country a service we can scarcely comprehend. This newspaper wishes to unreservedly apologise...

And then there was a photograph of a shadowy Raoul being escorted to the plane. And another headline.

Bring Her Home, Raoul.
We need her.

'Is that why you're really here?' Claire asked in a small voice. 'To...to bring me back?'

And Raoul set his laptop aside and turned to hold her. 'No,' he said, firmly and surely. 'The media's fickle. They might now have decided they love you, but *I* fell in love with you approximately two minutes after I met you, and I'm not fickle. Claire, I booked my plane ticket almost a week ago. What I'm doing has nothing to do with how my country's reacting to you now. It's all about loving you.'

'They think you're here persuading me to return.'

'That's because we haven't released a statement yet,' he told her. 'Henri made me wait until I was here, until I'd had time to ask you to marry me, before we made an official statement. He said—and he may be right—that if you told me to go to the devil then I might well decide to head back to Marétal with my tail between my legs.'

'And be a solitary prince forever?'

'Probably.' But he hugged her tighter. 'Luckily that's not an option. You've agreed. Do you think we could sneak out today and buy a ring?'

'Sneak out?'

'We could go out the back way. Get one of those nice tinted limos. Go somewhere innocuous and buy a diamond.'

She thought about it. There was a lot to be said for it.

We could go out the back way. Get one of those nice tinted limos. Go somewhere innocuous...'

Coward.

The word slammed into her head and stayed.

Coward.

She looked at Raoul—really looked at him. He was her soldier, her lover, her Prince.

He'd offered to give up his world for her.

He'd asked her to marry him and she'd said yes.

But had she said yes to Prince Raoul or had she said yes to the man she'd like him to be? A man disappearing into the shadows because she didn't have the courage to stand beside him?

She thought suddenly of that appalling time almost six months ago, when she'd been hounded by the thought of wrongful fraud charges. Running to Orcas Island.

Becoming a shadow.

She thought of the taunts of her childhood and how she'd hidden in her books. Keeping her head down. Being nothing. Hoping no one would notice.

She thought of her workplace, wearing black or beige. Making no waves. Cringing as she waited for criticism.

Coward.

'Raoul,' she said, in a voice that must belong to her but she barely recognised it. It was another woman's voice. Something inside her had shifted. Or come together.

Raoul met her gaze and she thought it was this man who'd changed her. Raoul had given her this. And she'd take it, she thought with sudden determination. Raoul loved her. What sort of gift was that? What was she about, continuing to run?

'Yes?'

He sensed something had changed. He knew her, this man. He knew her so well.

They could stand side by side forever.

'Would you help me bring Felicity to justice?' she asked, and he blinked.

'Felicity?' He looked confused—as well he might.

'She stole money from my law firm,' she said, clearly now, because suddenly her way was defined and there was no way she could deviate. 'I was blamed, but with decent lawyers I could prove it wasn't me. I chose not to make a fuss. That was partly because I didn't have the funds to fight, but I could have borrowed to do it. I chose not to. I chose to disappear. Felicity and her nasty friends counted on it. But suddenly... Raoul, I don't want to disappear any more, and I don't want an accusation of fraud hanging over my head. Even though they've hushed it up I won't accept it. Will you help me?'

'I...yes. Of course I will. Though maybe you should wait a little. For the next couple of weeks you'll be the target of media.'

'Then media might be able to help me. If an accusation is made, I'll defend myself.' She took a deep breath. 'If you're by my side.'

'You know I will be.'

'As the proprietor of Attack Dog Security?'

He smiled at that. 'We need to get Rocky out of quarantine first.'

It was harder to get Rocky back into Australia than it had been to get him to Marétal. He was currently one day into a hefty quarantine period.

'That's another thing,' she said diffidently. 'I don't want my dog locked up any more.'

'Australian quarantine is stringent,' he said, cautious now, not sure where she was going.

'But if we decided to get back on a plane tomorrow, to return to Marétal, then he'd spend only two more days in a cage.'

What followed was a moment's silence. No, make that more than a moment. It was long and it was filled with questions and it stretched on forever.

'*We?*' Raoul asked, and his voice sounded strange. 'If *we* decided?'

'I'm not sending Rocky back without me.' She hesitated, and then she placed the computer carefully out of the way, so there was nothing between them. Nothing at all. She took his hands in hers and held them tight. 'And I won't go back without you. But I will go back.'

'Why?' His voice was laced with strain.

'Because it's right,' she whispered. 'Because I know it's right. Because your place is there and my place is at your side.'

'Claire, there'll be…'

'Media. Intrusion. Lack of privacy. But, hey…' She suddenly cheered up. 'There'll also be an awesome hairstylist. She's lovely, and I bet as a princess I can have her do my hair every time we have a state occasion.'

'She can do it every day,' he said grandly. 'But, love…'

'Mmm?' She'd moved on. She was starting to think about personal hairstylists. And the palace gardens, which surely beat the rocks of Orcas Island. And a library. And chandeliers…

'What are you thinking?' he asked uneasily, and she grinned.

'If the Queen can have a chandelier in her bedroom I don't see why I can't have one.'

'You can have ten.' And then he reconsidered. 'But not as big as the one in the ballroom?'

'No?' She sounded gutted, and he laughed, and then he drew her to him and his face grew serious.

'Claire, what are you saying? You know I love you, but this is huge. You're a private person. You'll be in a goldfish bowl.'

'We can buy curtains.'

'Claire…'

'I just figured it out,' she said, cupping his face in her hands, holding him, loving him. 'It's taken me a while, but I have it. This courage thing… Do you remember in the water? I saved you and you saved me right back? As a team, imagine how much more we could save. Imagine how we could save each other.'

'We could do it here,' he said urgently. 'With our Killer Attack—'

'Don't tempt me.' She put a finger on his mouth, shushing him. 'I've been an idiot. If I have you beside me why do I need privacy? Why do I need anything but you? And you… Raoul, you're needed in Marétal. You know you are. I'll never forget that you've given me this choice, but if you stay here you'll worry about your country. You'll worry about your grandparents. You'll worry about security and whether your people can get legal assistance and proper education and healthcare. And, as much as I know that the Attack Dog Security team could do some vital work, keeping the citizens of Australia safe, I suspect that we could do more in Marétal. If we work together.'

There was another pause—a pause so long she didn't know how to break it.

Raoul's hands gripped hers so tightly they hurt.

'You'd do that?' he asked her in a voice choked with emotion. 'For me?'

'No.' She shook her head. 'I've been stupid. I've been a coward. And I didn't see I'd be doing it for *us*. I'm even thinking Cinders had a point, accepting her Prince's hand on the basis of one glass slipper—though I have to think that she was a wuss, staying in the kitchen waiting for him. I won't wait for you, Raoul. I want you *now*. I want you forever.'

How had things changed so fast? She didn't know. She would never afterwards be able to tell. But all she knew was that they had.

She wasn't a coward. She wasn't the illegitimate kid—the one dressed in secondhand clothes, trying to claw her way up through poverty. She wasn't anyone the Felicitys of this world could stomp over.

She was Claire, and she was loved by Raoul, she thought. She was loved by her man.

And then she forgot to think, because she was being kissed—kissed as she needed to be kissed, as she deserved to be kissed—and she kissed him back. And there was nothing else to be said for a very long time.

And afterwards—when the kiss was finally done, when there was room again for words between them—Raoul pushed her back and his dark eyes gleamed.

'Diamonds,' he told her, with all the authority of the Royal House of Marétal behind him. 'This very afternoon. Do you still want the back way and tinted limousines?'

'Not on your life,' she told him. 'I want a chariot or six. Where do you think we can find a pumpkin, a few mice and a fairy godmother?'

CHAPTER TWELVE

THEY WERE MARRIED six months later, with all the pomp and ceremony Queen Alicia could manage. She had decreed that a royal wedding must be a showcase of splendour, and so it was. Every dignitary in the land was there, plus as many of Europe's aristocracy as she'd been able to summon.

But no one had needed much summoning. This was a day of joy, and the world was waiting and willing to share.

The bride arrived at the cathedral in a magnificent, horse-drawn coach, with the Horseguards of Marétal parading before her. By Claire's side was King Marcus.

'A girl has to have someone to give her away,' Marcus had said, emerging from his library to give a decree of his own. 'You've almost single-handedly saved the royal family of Marétal. Unless there's someone else at hand to do it, it would be my very great honour to assist.'

And Claire had joyfully agreed.

Marcus was her future father-in-law.

Marcus was the King of Marétal.

Marcus was her ally and her friend.

She seemed to have lots of friends now, she thought, though she was still dubious about many.

There'd even been a fawning letter from one of the associates at her old law firm…

You always seemed such a loner, but I was thinking...we did enjoy shopping together. And I've always been on your side, even though I couldn't say. I needed my job too much. If you need a bridesmaid...

Claire most definitely didn't. That appalling time was best forgotten.

Thanks to Raoul's intervention, Felicity and her partner were now facing a hefty jail sentence, and there'd been an 'undisclosed' amount of compensation paid into Claire's bank account. There'd been media coverage of the entire case.

So now it could be forgotten—and today of all days who would think of it?

There were crowds lining the streets, smiling and cheering.

'Wave,' Marcus told her, and she thought of how anonymous she'd always wanted to be.

But she managed to wave, and Marcus waved, too, and she thought, *We're two of a kind. Two introverts in the royal spotlight.*

And then she stopped thinking, for they'd reached the cathedral. Henri was handing her down from the coach. Henri, too, had become a true friend, as had her gorgeous hairstylist, who was currently fussing over her train.

And then it was time.

The doors to the cathedral were flung wide. The sound of trumpets rose triumphantly to the skies.

'Ready?' Marcus asked.

She took a deep breath and nodded. They trod regally—as she'd practised—up the great steps, in through the nave.

The cathedral opened up before them, magnificent in its age and beauty. It was filled with every dignitary in the land, plus so many people who were Raoul's friends and who were becoming her friends.

Raoul stood at the altar. Beside him was Tom, owner of *Rosebud*—because Raoul had thought, Who else could be his best man? The soldier who'd lent him his unseaworthy boat, which had led to him being saved by Claire, was the obvious choice.

But Raoul had saved her back, Claire thought mistily as the sound of trumpets filled the cathedral, as the congregation rose to its feet, and as Raoul turned and smiled at her.

Raoul's smile…

That was what had got her into this mess, she thought. That was the whole trouble.

That was the whole joy.

He smiled, and the over-the-top setting was forgotten. She'd practised walking in this amazing dress, with its vast train, with its priceless adornments. She'd practised keeping step with Marcus. She'd even practised her vows.

But who could think of any of those things when

Raoul was standing at the end of the aisle waiting for her?

Raoul. Her heart. Her destiny.

He was in full royal regalia. He looked magnificent, but she wasn't seeing the uniform. She was only seeing Raoul.

Theirs wouldn't be a marriage like that of Marcus and Alicia, she thought mistily. Raoul wanted—needed—her to share his kingdom and of course she would.

For she wasn't unequal. She was loved. She and Raoul were meant to be forever and ever, she thought, and she managed a tremulous smile back at the man she loved with all her heart.

'You can do this,' Marcus whispered at her side, and she managed to smile at the old man, the King of Marétal.

'Of course I can,' she whispered back, and then there was nothing left to be said.

She made her way down the aisle to be married.

Surely there'd never been a more beautiful royal bride, Raoul thought as he watched Claire and his grandfather walk steadily along the aisle towards him. Even the Queen's eyes were misting with tears.

His beautiful Claire was coming to wed him.

By Raoul's feet sat Rocky. Claire had tried to train him to be the ring-bearer, but in rehearsals he'd proved unreliable to say the least.

'But he needs to be there,' Claire had said.

So they'd organised a velvet cushion to be placed front and centre. Claire had trained and trained him, and this morning a footman had taken him on a run that should exhaust the most exuberant dog. So he now lay by Raoul's side, looking as if butter wouldn't melt in his mouth.

But he was also watching Claire approach, and he wasn't totally to be trusted.

'Stay,' Raoul murmured as he stirred, and he looked up at Raoul and thankfully subsided. He wouldn't jump up on the royal bride.

'She's exquisite,' Tom breathed as Claire grew nearer. 'You lucky man.'

And that reminded Raoul of the final thing he had to do.

In his pocket was the tiny figure made of plastic building blocks. Herbert. Tom's good luck charm.

He hadn't admitted to Tom that he'd found him, but now it was time.

'This is yours,' he told Tom. He handed him over but his gaze didn't leave Claire.

'You found Herbert?' Tom stared down at the tiny figure in astonishment. 'My good luck Herbert?'

'I've had him and I've used him,' he told him. 'But as of today he's all yours. Use him wisely, my friend.'

Tom looked at him in bemusement, and then pocketed Herbert safely beside the royal wedding rings. There were things he wanted to ask, but now wasn't the time.

For Claire had reached her Raoul, and Claire was smiling and smiling, and even a tough Special Forces soldier like Tom was finding it hard not to choke up.

'My Claire,' Raoul whispered, taking her hands and drawing her forward. 'My love. Are you ready to be married?'

And Claire's smile softened to a tenderness that must melt the hardest of hearts.

'How can you doubt it, my love?' she whispered. 'Indeed I am.'

Marétal's first legal assistance office was opened six months later. A small, nondescript building, set in the part of the capital where it was most needed, it seemed a bizarre setting for the fanfare that went with the opening. For not only were the King and Queen present, but so were His Royal Highness Crown Prince Raoul and his beautiful wife the Princess Claire.

Claire wore a turquoise and white dress from one of Australia's leading designers. For this she was criticised in the media the following day—*Support Our Industries!*

The article beside it also wondered why the royal family was always accompanied by a nondescript fox terrier, when everyone knew the royal dog of Marétal should be the Marétal Spaniel.

Claire read those articles early. For once she'd woken before Raoul and had fetched the papers to read in bed. She smiled when she read them. She then hugged the dog she'd graciously admitted to the royal bedroom—because a woman needed some company before her husband woke.

She thought briefly about the articles and decided that she liked her turquoise and white designer frock very much, regardless of who had designed it. And she loved her dog.

And then she forgot all about them.

For her days were too busy for her to be bothered with criticism. She had better things to be doing than worrying about the day's press.

Things like lying in the arms of her husband. Things like living happily-ever-after.

Finally he was waking.

'What are you doing, woman?'

Raoul's voice was a sleepy murmur as he tugged her down against him. Passion was never far away. Love was for always.

'I'm thinking I might get my toenails painted,' she told him, kissing him with all the tenderness he deserved. 'Louise knows someone who can paint intricate designs on individual toes. Does that seem a good idea?'

There was a moment's pause, and then a fast re-arrangement of the bedding while the toes in question were examined.

'They seem good to me now,' he told her at last. 'I like them as they are.'

'They seem like a bare canvas.'

'What would you like on them?'

'Storks,' she said complacently. 'I'm wearing open-toed sandals to my next three functions. I'm wondering if the media will pick it up.'

There was another pause. A longer one.

'Storks?' he said at last, and she chuckled.

'Yep. Mind you, if I do it today I'll need to fit the appointment in well before my meeting with the Chief Justice. It wouldn't do to appear before His Lordship with not-yet-dried toes.'

'I guess it wouldn't.'

But Raoul had ceased his toe inspection. He sat up and gazed at her in bemusement.

Claire smiled at him and thought she'd never seen him look sexier. Mind, it could be the early-morning sun reflected from the crystal chandelier above her head.

No, she thought dreamily. He'd looked just as wonderful back on Orcas Island. Her soldier. Her sailor. Her love.

'Are we by any chance going to have a baby?' Raoul demanded at last, in a voice that was just a tiny bit strangled.

'We might be.'

If she sounded like the cat that had got the cream, who could blame her?

'You're pregnant!'

'Only a bit.'

Ten weeks. It was time she told him—probably more than time—but life was busy, and he'd fuss, and they were so gloriously happy how could anything make them *more* happy?

But she was wrong. What crossed Raoul's face was a flash of joy so profound she felt her eyes welling with emotion. With love.

'Claire...'

'Papa,' she said, and then she could say no more. She was gathered into his arms and held.

So in the end she had to delay having her toes painted with little storks, and she was sadly late for her meeting with the Chief Justice.

'There's no use being royal if I can't issue a royal decree,' Raoul declared. 'And this morning I decree that my wife will lie in my arms until she's listened to every reason why she's cherished. Are there any objections?'

'No, Your Highness,' she whispered as he folded her into him. 'I can't think of a single one.'

* * * * *